1

HACKER SALVATION

WHITE HAT SECURITY, BOOK 7

LINZI BAXTER

Hacker
Betoued
1-24-23

Hacker Salvation
White Hat Security, Book 7
Copyright © 2019 by Linzi Baxter
Cover Artist: Cassy Roop, Pink Ink Designs
Cover Model: Roddy
Cover Photographer: Wander Aguiar
Edited by: Red Adept Editing

BLURB

A marriage of convenience...

Annabella is tired of being used. Used as an A-list arm ornament. Used for her fame and her money. When she's done filming her latest movie, she plans to play the ultimate acting role—a marriage in name only. It's not love, but at least she'll have peace.

Those plans come to a shrieking halt when she finds her home stained with blood, her fiancé missing —and a police officer reading her Miranda rights. The rescuer who walks into the station isn't her friend Daisy, but a six-foot-four, mouthwatering wall of muscle who rivets her gaze.

An attraction deeper than blood and bone...

One look at Annabella's vulnerable, tear-streaked face, and John Waters wants nothing more than to clear a path for her. Through a sea of reporters to a waiting car. Through any danger to safety. Through her tangled emotions, straight to his arms.

In what universe is a broken, ex-Navy SEAL in the same league with silver-screen perfection? He should be slamming the brakes on his desire, right effing now. But to keep her safe from mounting danger, he has to keep her close. And that's the biggest danger of all—to his heart.

ANNABELLA

"Ma'am, put down the knife."

I looked up from the bloody knife in my hands to see a Los Angeles County sheriff's deputy standing at the entrance to Nate's bathroom. The man wore the typical law-enforcement uniform of a tan button-down shirt and green pants. His aviator glasses sat on top of his short, spiky blond hair. He rested his hand on the butt of the gun in his holster.

This might be bad. Really bad.

I shut my eyes and hoped he was a figment of my imagination. When I opened my eyes again, he was still there in my house. "Why are you in my house?" I asked quickly. "I never heard the doorbell ring. Why did you let yourself in?"

My eyes darted to where the deputy tapped his

finger on the top of his gun. "Your housekeeper let us in. Now please put down the knife and step back from the crime scene."

The words "crime scene" slowly sank in as my eyes took a second look around the bathroom. Needing to explain more, I stepped forward without putting the knife down.

The deputy drew his gun from his belt. "You need to put the weapon down."

When I'd gotten home last night, I had been exhausted from working a thirteen-hour day on the set of *Last Love,* my latest film. Nate and I had gotten into an argument over him not helping with the wedding plans. His breath had smelled like alcohol, and his clothes had smelled like another man's cologne. Earlier in the day, Nate had sent me a text, saying he'd gotten an email with our results and couldn't wait to show me mine. I'd rushed home after work to find him not home yet. We'd made plans to look at our 23andMe reports. Nate had told me he was going to print off the results so we could look at them over a glass of wine. I didn't know much about my father's side, so I chose to leave my name public when I filled out the documents. I couldn't wait to find out if I had family I didn't know about. Most people would look at the results online, but Nate and I wanted to read ours together, so he was supposed to bring them both home tonight for us to look at. Instead, he'd chosen to ditch me to go out to the bar. I'd gone to bed, and he'd left. This morning after I'd woken up, I noticed he hadn't come back.

Nate and I had been friends since grade school. We'd stayed close even though he had gone to Harvard Law School and I had pursued acting at Stella Adler Academy of Acting and Theatre. Still, we'd always made time for each other. Ever since we were little, I'd known he was gay.

His family, on the other hand, had a different idea for him. He was to marry the daughter of another successful family to help grow his parents' business. They owned a law firm. Last year, Nate had refused to marry who they wanted, and he'd told them he was gay. Two days later, he came home with a broken arm and a black eye. When I asked what had happened, he just asked if I would marry him.

Over the years, I'd gotten sick of men using me to advance their careers in showbiz. So I'd agreed to be his wife on paper and live with him. Nate was my best friend. He'd never used me to get his name in the tabloids.

After my long workday, I'd driven to the house we shared. Nate's car had been sitting in the driveway. I'd screamed his name as I walked around the house. A smudge of blood had caught my eye when I passed his bedroom. I walked through his bedroom to see where the blood came from and found his bathroom covered with blood. I thought he'd gotten hurt and someone had taken him to the hospital.

"I won't repeat myself," the deputy said firmly. "You need to put the knife down."

I laid the heavy silver carving knife on the marble countertop and stepped forward, only to slip in the blood. A screech left my mouth as I flailed backward, trying to grab anything on my way down. When my ass hit the marble floor, the impact knocked the breath out of me.

I slowly sat up. My once-white dress was red, and my hands were stained with blood. I gripped the counter and pulled myself off the ground. I was leaving a trail of bloody handprints on the bathroom counter. The sheriff stood at the door, watching my every move.

I glared at him. "Can you please give me a moment?" My tailbone hurt from hitting the hard floor.

The sheriff frowned at me. "The sheriff's office is not going to treat you any differently than a normal criminal. We don't care how famous you are. Please step out of the bathroom."

I didn't know if it was from the stress of the day or having a gun pointed at me, but my eyes started to water. It felt as though my life was about to be turned upside down. I tentatively stepped forward, trying not to slip on the floor again. When I reached the doorway, the sheriff grabbed me by the arm.

I pulled back. "Wait! I need to wipe my feet off."

The officer yanked me forward. "We don't have time."

My blood-covered foot sank into the white plush carpet. Each step left a bloody footprint. I glanced around Nate's room one more time, hoping he would jump out and scream, "Gotcha!" But he didn't. I blinked a couple of times to clear my vision.

When we reached the grand staircase, which opened to the entryway, I noticed two officers talking to our new cleaner, whom Nate had hired a week ago. She turned and pointed at me. I hadn't spoken to the new housekeeper yet, but if I had to guess, she was in her late sixties. She was wearing a pair of jeans and a T-shirt. Her gray hair was pulled up into a loose bun. But it was the glint in her eyes that made me think she knew more than she was letting on.

"Wait." I stopped the deputy before he pulled me down the stairs. He turned his narrowed gray eyes on me. "I need to change. I can't walk around covered in blood."

The deputy pinched the bridge of his nose. "I don't like repeating myself, Ms. Harper. You will not get any special favors because of who you are. You need to be processed now since you decided to contaminate the crime scene."

I took a couple of deep breaths. "Why do you keep

saying crime scene? Who is missing? Why are you here? I don't understand."

He sneered as he spoke. "If you would follow me downstairs, we can talk about your missing fiancé."

My feet faltered under his words, and I fell forward but caught myself on the railing before I went headfirst down the stairs. I couldn't hold back the tears. "Nate," I whispered. This couldn't be happening. Last night, we'd had an ugly fight. We had both said things we couldn't take back. But he was my best friend. Even though I was mad at him, I would never want him to go missing.

With each step I took down the white marble staircase, my mind swirled with questions. *Is Nate really hurt? Why did the housekeeper call the cops without talking to me?*

By the time we reached the entryway, my new housekeeper, Ms. Orchard, was sobbing into a handkerchief. She looked up at me, hatred showing in her eyes. The older lady blinked the emotion away so fast, I almost thought for a second that she wasn't up to something.

"I can't believe you killed Nate."

I held up my bloody hands. "Wait one second. Why are you accusing me of killing my fiancé and best friend. And why does everyone think he's dead?"

Ms. Orchard's lips turned into a nasty grin. "I saw you guys fight last night and turned over the video to the police. How convenient he changed his will early this week and you get everything. Two days later, he dies. Don't try to hide the fact that you murdered your fiancé. I already gave the police the video."

One of the deputies I hadn't met yet shifted to his other foot. "Ms. Harper, where have you been all day?"

I took a deep breath. "I was at work. You can call the director of *Last Love* or ask anyone on set. I was at work all day."

The front doors opened, and three men in CSI jackets walked in. Deputy Charles led the group of men up the staircase.

"Can you guys just walk in and take over?" I asked.

When the deputy shifted, I could see his last name printed on his shirt. Deputy Judges eyed the group as they disappeared down the upstairs hallway. "Nate's dad called the sheriff this morning to report his son didn't show up to work. He said that was unusual."

I wanted to scream that was a lie. Nate was notorious for missing work. Something strange was happening.

The deputy continued. "Nate's dad supports the sheriff's department and donates money each year to our causes. So we decided to check it out. When we were on our way, Ms. Orchard called to tell us she saw you with Nate's blood on your hands."

"I can tell you for sure she never saw me with blood on my hands. The videotape should've shown you that as well. I was in the bathroom for only a minute before you showed up. Hell, look at the footage. I was only home a few minutes before you guys came busting into my house, uninvited. Check the house video cameras."

The deputy crossed his arms over his chest. "Someone deleted all the camera footage from your house."

"Then how is there video from mine and Nate's fight last night?"

Ms. Orchard pulled out her phone. "I forgot something at the house, and when I came back, I saw the two of you fighting, and you were so mad. You seemed like you would hurt him, so I took video."

Every staff member signed a nondisclosure agreement and a contract. She was in breach of contract for filming anything that happened inside our house. Tabloids paid big money for the scoops on celebrities' homes, and Nate had reassured me Ms. Orchard would be clear. If that video got out, it would destroy Nate more than me.

"Okay, Deputy Judges, if you saw the video, I would be cleared. Why aren't you looking for the person who gave Nate the black eye and asking about the reason we fought?" I turned toward Ms. Orchard. "You are fired and need to get off my property immediately. If the police need to talk to you, they can take you out of here. As of this second, you are no longer under my employment or Nate's."

Ms. Orchard stuck her hands on her hips. "You can't fire me. I'm to take care of this house and make sure everything runs for Nate. If you didn't kill him and he's coming back, I need to make sure he has everything."

I rolled my eyes. "Well, you called the cops and said I killed him. So you must think he's dead. If you read your contract correctly, you would know I can fire you. And you are going to be receiving a lawsuit for filming our private moments, because I can tell you one thing —I'm innocent and won't stop until I find Nate. Now get out."

When she didn't move, I looked at the deputy and raised my brow. He motioned for his partner, who escorted the ex-employee out.

"Now, can you tell me what's next?" I asked. "I haven't seen Nate since last night. Why does his dad think he's missing? Nate is known for going off on vacation without telling his dad. And will someone please let me change and wash my hands?"

"It would be easier to do this at the station. After we process you, we can ask a few more questions."

I looked back up the stairs, where the CSI unit was. "Why can't they do my process?"

The deputy let out an aggravated sigh before speaking into his hand radio. "Jake, I need you to send a tech down to process Ms. Harper's clothing." A few seconds later one of the CSI men came downstairs and processed me. He scraped under my nails and swabbed my hands. I asked if I could grab different clothes from upstairs, but they wouldn't let me go back up. The tech called down to process my clothing pulled out a pair of blue scrubs from his bag. The scrubs were in a clear plastic bag. I went into the bathroom, changed, and gave my white dress to one of the CSI guys.

My head started to pound from the stress, and my stomach growled. I hadn't eaten all day. We had been trying to finish up a scene on *Last Love* and had all agreed to work through lunch. I'd planned to rush home then head over to Daisy's grand opening.

Daisy's open house for her women's shelter was today. Thinking of what my friend had overcome brought a smile to my face. Fifteen years ago, she was kidnapped and held captive for ten years. Daisy had come back to California for the first time since her rescue five years ago after she'd started dating Neal and Aaron. They'd wanted her to come out to California for a trip. When she and her men came, people from her past had come back and wanted her again, and some crazy people had kidnapped her. Not all the men from her original kidnapping had been put away ten years ago. Now she and her two men, Aaron and Neal, were opening a women's shelter to help women who were down on their luck. Even though I hadn't talked to Daisy over the last fifteen years, I still considered her one of my girlfriends. So when she'd come out to Los Angeles a few months ago, we caught up, and our friendship picked up from where it had left off fifteen years ago. After living in Hollywood for so long, I was used to people wanting something from me or being my friend until they reached a goal. But Daisy wasn't like that. She only wanted to help people.

One of her future husband's Aaron and I had appeared together in the movie *Running from Justice*. I still couldn't believe he had decided to leave the movie industry. Aaron, Neal, and Daisy were going to live their lives mostly in Ft. Lauderdale. They still planned to come to California and work at the shelter. The new shelter in Los Angeles would be a sister shelter to the Ross Women's Outreach Center in Ft. Lauderdale. The Ross family had opened the outreach center in Ft. Lauderdale ten years ago. Kat, Aaron's sister in-law had taken over running the outreach center for the family.

I couldn't help but glance at the clock on the far wall. The grand opening of Daisy's shelter had started twenty minutes ago. "What is the next step, and when are you going to look for Nate?"

"We need you to come down to the station and make an official statement," the deputy said.

"Can I do it tomorrow? I have somewhere to be." Neal and Aaron both had connections and would be able to help me figure out what the hell was going on.

The deputy narrowed his eyes at me. "Your fiancé

might be dead, and you want to put off making your statement?"

"Fine. Can we leave now?"

He radioed the men upstairs. "Taking Ms. Harper to the station for her official report."

FOR THE FIFTH TIME, I glanced at the clock in the Los Angeles sheriff's office. Sheriff Clark wanted to speak with me. I had given my statement an hour ago, but I sat in the sheriff's office, waiting for him to show up. Pictures of awards and medals covered the wall. On his desk sat a photo of him with the governor of California.

The deputy had taken my phone when we'd left my house, so I hadn't called or talked to anyone. Daisy would be worried when I didn't show up. We had talked at lunch, and I'd told her about my plan to run home before I went to the shelter. I hoped the tabloids wouldn't get the scent of the scandal before I could speak with her.

The door to the office opened, and a man who looked to be in his late sixties walked in and sat down on the leather high-back chair. He crossed his arms and leaned back. "Your alibi for today checks out, but the judge still thinks you had something to do with Nate missing." I couldn't help but grind my teeth.

Nate's dad was throwing his money around to get his way. "The judge has decided to pull your passport until we get more information on Nate's whereabouts."

"I don't have my passport on me. The deputy made me leave everything at home."

"You have forty-eight hours to bring your passport back here." The sheriff sat back in his chair, watching my every move. I felt like he was waiting for me to make a move or confess to the murder.

"Can the deputy grab my passport when he takes me home? I don't want to come back to the police station. The media is going to have a field day with this."

The sound of him tapping his pencil on the desk echoed through the small office. "First off, we aren't giving you a ride home. Secondly, you should've thought about the consequences when you killed Nate."

I ground my teeth together. "I didn't kill Nate. How am I supposed to get home? I don't have my cell phone or purse."

Sheriff Clark shrugged. "I will let you use my phone to call someone."

Nate had changed his will two days prior to his disappearance, and because of that, the police thought I was the main suspect. He'd done it without telling his family. From what I'd overheard the deputies saying, his dad had seen the paperwork for the will earlier in the day then went looking for his son. When he couldn't find him, he called the police.

Luckily, I found someone to come get me. "Can I go?"

Sheriff Clark studied me for a moment. "For now. Nevertheless, don't go far and make sure you have your passport here within forty-eight hours, or we will issue a warrant for your arrest. We might have more questions."

2

JOHN

I groaned as my phone vibrated in my pocket. I considered ignoring the call, but I had already dismissed the last few calls. I knew my sister would show up outside my hotel room in Los Angeles if I didn't answer soon. Last night, I'd slipped and said that Annabella Harper would be at Daisy's grand opening. Normally, I would've done anything to make my baby sister happy, but I froze every time Annabella walked into the room. She was breathtaking. Luckily for me, she hadn't shown up yet, so I wouldn't have to approach her.

"Is she there?"

"Hey, pip-squeak. No, she is not here yet."

Addie huffed on the other end of the phone. "I'm thirty-five years old. Stop calling me pip-squeak."

"You are my baby sister and will always be a pip-squeak."

"By two minutes. Two minutes doesn't really count. I still think the doctor lied on who was born first."

"The doctor didn't lie." I grabbed another balloon and filled it with helium. "I thought you were meeting a new client today."

"I took the case, but I ended up interviewing him over the phone." Addie owned a PI firm in Boston. A few weeks ago, a little girl had gone missing in the Boston area, and her dad had recently scheduled an appointment with Addie. We'd discussed the case last night when I called to tell her I was in Los Angeles for the grand opening of Daisy's women's shelter.

No matter how hard I tried to get Addie to change careers, she wouldn't. When we were younger, our mother disappeared. We still didn't know what had happened to her. Now my sister spent her time taking cases that required her to look for missing people. She used those cases to fund her search for our mother. No matter how many times I asked, she wouldn't stop searching.

Our dad had turned to drugs and alcohol when our mom went missing. Addie and I had ended up raising ourselves. I'd gone into the military the day I turned eighteen so I could send Addie to college. I couldn't be prouder of my sister, who had double majored in criminal justice and cybersecurity.

A few years ago, I worked an op, and an IUD exploded next to me. I reached up and ran my hand along the scar on my face. It wasn't the only reminder of the day one of my men had betrayed me. My leg ached where the Navy doctors had pulled out the shrapnel. The Navy had discharged me when I lost part of the feeling in my leg. I joined Blackwood Security in Ft. Lauderdale after I received my discharge papers. I'd asked Addie to come work for Brock, but she wouldn't leave Boston. She said she would move once she found out what had happened to our mom.

I missed being around my sister. "Are you still sure you won't move to Ft. Lauderdale? I know Brock would love to have you."

Addie let out an aggravated sigh. "You know I can't move until I solve Mom's case." She took a deep breath. "Don't start. I know Mom went missing twenty years ago."

"Okay." I blew up another balloon. Brock stood across from me, blowing up balloons. His wife, Jessica, sat in the chair next to us and tied the balloons after we filled them up. Brock raised a brow at my conversation, but I waved him off and continued. "I just miss my baby sister."

Brock and I had gone through basic training together, and he knew how much my sister meant to me. Yes, our father was still alive, but neither of us had talked to him since the day we'd turned eighteen.

Addie had used my signing bonus to head off to school, and I had gone into the Navy.

"You act like we never talk," Addie teased. "We talk every day, John. Now, don't forget to FaceTime me when Annabella shows up."

I glanced toward the front doors of the women's shelter. Six women who Daisy had helped rescue from a sex trade were assisting her in putting balloons around the entrance.

I had met Annabella a couple of times since flying out to Los Angeles to help Daisy with the new shelter. Daisy meant a lot to me. Five years ago, Brock, Sam, and I had rescued her from a man who'd held her captive for ten years. Three months ago was the first time Daisy had stepped foot back in California since she'd been rescued. Her time back hadn't gone as planned, and someone from her past had tried to make her pay. She'd helped expose the sex-trade industry and was still running from her old captor. Because of her bravery, six women were safe, and now she was trying to help others.

I grabbed another balloon from the pile. If I didn't cut the conversation with Addie soon, I would never get her off the phone. "Look, I need to help set up. If or when Annabella shows up, I will call you."

Addie's voice turned sweet. "You're the best big brother."

"You don't need to suck up. I already told you I

would call you when she shows up." I would do anything to make my sister happy. Annabella was one of the people she looked up to for her charity work. One of Annabella's charities donated money to people with agoraphobia. I couldn't help but close my eyes as I thought of my mother, who'd suffered from agoraphobia. She'd barely been able to leave the house, and that was one of the reason's Addie believed someone had taken Mom and she hadn't run away.

The other reason Addie cared about the cause was because she had borderline agoraphobia. It was something she didn't like to talk about, but I'd picked up the cues early. When we'd spoken the night before, she had said she planned to meet her new client at a local coffee shop. But that morning, she said she'd talked to him over the phone. Addie hired qualified people to collect data. She analyzed the cases and came up with scenarios.

Silence filled the line for a second. When Addie finally spoke, her voice shook slightly. "Um, John, I had someone else show up to the house today as well."

The hairs on my neck instantly stood up. "Who?" It came out as more of a demand than a question.

"Dad."

I loosened my grip on the balloon, and it flew through the air, letting out a screeching noise. My words were stuck in the back of my throat.

"John?"

"What did he want?" I growled.

"To talk." Addie's voice was soft. "He's sober now and wants to see you too."

"Pass." I ran my hand through my hair and noticed Brock had stopped blowing up balloons. In fact, everyone had stopped working and was staring at me. "Hey, Addie, I need to go. If Annabella shows up, I'll call you." I might've upset my sister, but I didn't have time to process the info that my dad had shown back up after fifteen years. He had checked out many years before Addie and I left the house.

She sniffled. "Don't be like that, John. He's all the family we have left."

It bothered me when she was upset. I sighed and rested my hip against the table. "I need time to process what you said. I'll give you a call back soon, pip-squeak."

"Okay, big bro. Talk to you soon."

"Bye." I clicked off the phone and shoved it in my pocket.

Brock was still staring at me. Jessica and everyone else had gone back to work. But my boss knew something was wrong. "What's going on, John?"

"My dad showed up at Addie's house this morning."

"Fuck." Brock's voice was deep and full of concern. "Do you want me to send Mia up there? I know your sister knows who she is." Everyone knew about my sister's agoraphobia, and she was nervous around people she didn't know.

"I will talk with her tonight, but we need to be here for Daisy. This is more important at the moment. When I talk to her later, I will ask her if she wants me to send someone up there. She probably won't want anyone."

"We could send someone just to keep an eye on her," Brock suggested.

"I'm not going to lie to my sister. Maybe we start looking into my dad and see if he's stopped drinking and gambling. I don't want Addie to let him back into her life and for him to let her down again." There were many times Dad's bookies would show up to the house, demanding money. I worried Addie would fall for some sad story and give him any money he asked for.

Brock rolled his eyes. "Your dad has lived in the same house since you were a kid. He sobered up three years ago and works as an accountant for a locally owned firm. I haven't seen anything out of the ordinary."

I didn't know if I should be happy or mad that my friend had looked into my dad. "Do you make it a habit of watching everyone's family members?"

Jessica looked up. "Oh, he watches out for everyone he cares about. Haven't you ever looked at his monitor on the right wall? It's his running board of everyone.

Last week, Mia had a date, and Brock checked him out. Mia cussed up a storm when she noticed his name on the monitor."

Brock shrugged. "I'm not going to stop taking care of the people I care about."

"Dude, a heads-up would be nice."

"Oh, then you should know—I used your computer the other day and checked your internet history," Jessica said. "You're normally so quiet, and I wanted to know what to get you for your birthday. I found out you like to look up Annabella."

Sometimes having close friends was a pain in the ass. "Dude, you both need to stay out of my personal life until I ask. You could've asked what I wanted. Guns, ammo, knives. See? The list is short. Furthermore, I only looked her up because Addie wouldn't stop talking about her charity."

"Are you talking about the charity she donates to that offers support to people with agoraphobia?" Jessica asked. "Did you know one point eight million Americans over the age of eighteen suffer? Does your sister have pain—"

Brock put a hand over his wife's mouth. "Why don't you go help Daisy out? People are starting to come in." He took his hand away from her mouth, but Jessica just chewed on her lip and stared at him. "Jess, let me talk with John. I promise you can do research later."

Jessica leaned in a gave Brock a kiss before she went to the front to help women check in.

Brock looked after his wife then turned and smirked at me. "She means well, man. When she finds something new to research, she wants to ask more questions to compile with the research she finds."

I was used to Jessica's quirks. The woman knew more about numbers and statistics than I could've ever imagined. Her need for knowledge sometimes took over, and she didn't filter her words. "It's no problem, but you need to stay out of my private life."

Brock gave me a brotherly pat on the back. "Let's grab a soda and get out of the way."

I glanced around as the room started to fill up. A new woman walking into the center was giving Brock and me an odd look. I was used to it with the scar that ran down the side of my face.

Brock led us over to the kitchen in the back. "You know you could talk to her. She will be here today."

"I wasn't stalking her. Addie wants to meet her. I researched her a little so I could ask her to FaceTime with Addie. Secondly, she's getting married."

"Not so sure she's marrying Nate for the right reasons." When I leveled a look at Brock, he continued. "Daisy mentioned something the other day about how she was worried, so I might've looked into it."

I didn't care what her reason was for marrying Nate. I would never go after a woman if she were engaged, even if it was for convenience. Plus, Annabella was a drop-dead gorgeous superstar. I couldn't think of one reason why she would like a scarred ex-seal.

"Doesn't matter. She's engaged."

Brock took a sip of his Coke and glanced over to where Jessica was laughing with two women I'd never met. "When you find the one, things change. And I want you to have that. You deserve to be happy."

Jessica glanced in our direction and waved Brock over.

He set his drink down. "Don't let life pass you by." Brock turned and walked toward Jessica with a smile across his face.

I realized I had gone through the motions of life the past few years. I knew sleeping with a new sub at Club Sanctorum every time I went left me empty. Maybe I would take Brock up on his advice and find someone.

A picture of Annabella in a silver dress flashed through my mind. Her blond locks fell past her shoulders. The woman was gorgeous, and her fiancé was equally handsome. Nate stood next to her in the photo, dressed in a black tux. His blue eyes were piercing. No matter how hot she was, though, she was off-limits and out of my league. My hands started to sweat as I thought about approaching her and asking her to talk to my sister.

Fuck that. I was an ex-SEAL, and she was a woman. I would ask her the quick favor. The worst she could say was no. Daisy always talked about how nice she was. But she'd said Annabella was going to show up earlier. The doors had opened an hour ago, and the sexy actress still wasn't there.

The words "drama queen" came to mind. I might've cyberstalked her a little, and people reported that she had to have things her way, or she would throw a fit. Maybe she wasn't all Daisy had talked her up to be.

As if she knew I was thinking about her, Daisy caught sight of me and headed over. She wrapped her arms around my waist and laid her head on my chest. "Have I ever said how much I appreciated you over the years, John?"

I awkwardly patted her back as her two men, Neal and Aaron, shot daggers in my direction. "Anyone would've done what I did. Now, you want to tell me what brought on the hug. Don't get me wrong—I like it —but I think your men are going to be over here soon if you don't let go."

Daisy stepped back and rolled her eyes. "This wouldn't have been possible if you and Sam hadn't rescued me from that asshole five years ago. And you flew across the country to help me with the opening."

The place looked amazing. The ten-thousand-foot building had classrooms, play areas, and sleeping quarters for women and kids trying to get back on their feet. I remembered times when my dad would lock Addie and me out of the house, and we would end up at a shelter. This place was like the Hilton compared to where we'd stayed.

I cleared my throat. "I will always be there for you, Daisy."

She started to reply, but her phone rang. She pulled it out and frowned as she looked at the screen. Then she tapped the phone and pressed it to her ear. "Where are you, Annabella?"

I couldn't hear the reply, but Daisy's eyes went wide. "They took you downtown?" she screeched.

By the time Daisy was done with her brief conversation, Neal, Brock, and Aaron stood around the kitchen island. Daisy told us that her friend was at the sheriff's station. Annabella's fiancé might be dead.

3

ANNABELLA

I could always count on Daisy. Uber had been my first idea, but I already heard the clicks of the cameras outside. Daisy's friend and ex-boss who owns a mercenary company was in town, and she'd told me he would send someone to help get me through the crowds. Now I just had to sit and wait, which wasn't easy to do given my location and the circumstances. I wasn't on some Hollywood set. There were genuine criminals in this place. But I wasn't one of them.

The sheriff had kicked me out of his office as soon as I finished making my call. The deputy from earlier had then escorted me to the waiting area. Everyone was staring at me, wondering why I was there. Deputy Charles hadn't let me grab my purse or phone before we'd left my house. Now I sat there, waiting for Daisy. I was not ready to face the million or so reporters on the other side of the door, who were anticipating my exit.

At one point I snapped at a little kid running around the waiting area. The mother whipped around and glared at me. As a star, I was unaccustomed to that kind of treatment. People regularly went out of their way to make me feel comfortable. Instead, the sheriff was trying to make an example out of me.

The front desk clerk mumbled something under her breath that I was too angry to even pay attention to. Then she turned to another guard, and they both looked in my direction and laughed. They didn't stop the paparazzi when they'd tried to come in. It was like the officers wanted my face plastered across the tabloids.

I tried to look calm, cool, and collected, but the whole situation was trying on me. I was in absolute danger of being photographed dressed down.

I hoped that Daisy would hurry up and get there. I'd never been taken down to the sheriff's station before. I shouldn't be there. All I could do was think about what had happened to cause me to end up there. None of it made any sense, not the housekeeper taking video or Nate missing. I prayed the blood in the upstairs bathroom wasn't his. I didn't know what I would do if I lost my best friend even though I was pissed as hell at him.

Finally, the doors to the waiting area opened, and

in walked a six-foot-four muscular man. He reminded me of the men Daisy talked about. He had on a pair of dark denim jeans and a white button-down shirt. The sleeves were rolled up, showing off the man's arms. Tattoos lined his biceps, adding to his sex appeal. I licked my lips. His hair was pulled back. He scanned the room until his eyes landed on me. At least I thought they did—it was difficult to tell because of the aviator glasses he was wearing.

With a couple of steps, he was by my side. He raised his glasses, and his deep-gray eyes hypnotized me. "Annabella, my name is John Waters. We've met a couple times. Daisy sent me to pick you up."

I didn't remember meeting him before. The man was sexy as hell. I would have remembered if he'd walked into a room. My mind was going a million miles a minute, and I wanted out of the sheriff's station. It wasn't that I was ungrateful Mr. Waters had come to get me, but I really needed to see my friend as soon as possible.

"Where's Daisy?" I blurted out.

"Waiting in the car. I'll take you to her."

Tears began to stream down my face, and I finally managed to say what I should've opened with. "Thank you." I felt like a broken woman. This was all more than I could handle at the moment.

"Here." John pulled off his leather jacket and handed it to me. "There are a lot of reporters out there.

When I open the door, stay next to me, and I will make a path. If you want to, cover your head with the jacket."

Everything seemed so unreal. I nodded and followed John to the door. When he pulled the handle of the door back, cameras blinded me with their flashes. Everyone was yelling my name, asking why I was taken in and where Nate was. I wished I knew. Not wanting my face plastered across all the gossip rags, I put John's jacket over my head then grabbed the back of his shirt and held on. With each step we took, the crowd became more restless. John reached back and grabbed my hand. I expected his hands to be rough and calloused. Instead, his hand was soft.

When we reached the sidewalk, Neal, one of Daisy's future husbands, jumped out of the black Escalade parked along the sidewalk and opened the back door. When we were within feet of the vehicle, John grabbed me around the waist and pushed me into the waiting SUV. The flashing lights and yells intensified with each step. John jumped in next to me and pulled the door shut. Even with the door closed and the blackout tint on the windows, the paparazzi continued to rain down questions.

At the top of the stairs to the station stood the officer who'd brought me in. His arms were crossed, and his sunglasses made it impossible to see his eyes. But his rigid stance and body language suggested he was glaring at our car.

"Are you okay?" Daisy asked as she wrapped her arms around me.

I shifted in the leather seat. "I don't know what I'm going to do."

Neal cleared his throat from the front seat, his eyes meeting mine through the review mirror. "Don't worry Annabella, Brock is meeting us at the house and we will figure everything out." John shifted in the seat next to me.

We were silent as we rode to the house Daisy shared with her men. Neal said not to worry, but he wasn't the one being accused of killing someone. Even worse, I was accused of killing my best friend. Aaron and Neal were in the front seat, while Daisy and I hugged each other throughout the entire ride in the back seat. John sat next to me. I could feel his body heat. He sat with his arms crossed and stared out the window.

I was struggling not to cry anymore. "Daisy, I'm sorry to pull you away from your opening. You can drop me off at my house, and you can go back." Earlier, I had panicked when the deputy said I had to go to the sheriff's office, and I hadn't known who to call. Asking Daisy to leave her special day was selfish of me, and I felt evil for doing it.

Daisy rolled her eyes. "Don't worry about it. We were already open for a while, and I got to meet a lot of the new girls. Kat, my sister-in-law, runs the sister shelter back in Ft. Lauderdale. She and her husband have it under control. Brock and Jessica are meeting us back at our house so we can figure out a game plan. Kat and Antonio will stay and work the shelter with the staff."

I let her words sink in. It was nice to have someone look out for me without wanting something in return. No one in Hollywood ever did anything without an ulterior motive or the promise of some type of gain. I could've called my manager, but I was worried he would turn the whole mess into some kind of publicity. All I wanted was to find Nate and figure out what had happened. He couldn't be dead. Even though I had been mad at him last night, I'd never wanted him to die.

"Okay, but I can go home."

John's deep, gravelly voice startled me. "I talked with the sheriff's office on our way over to pick you up. Your house hasn't been released yet. You might be able to get back in tomorrow."

I laid my head back against the leather seat and listened as everyone talked around me. I closed my eyes, hoping that when I opened them, this nightmare would be over and I could go back to my customary life. I didn't even want to look at my phone. More than likely, I had twenty missed calls from my manager and double that from the producer of the movie I was working on. The contract for the film had stipulations about being arrested. I'd never imagined it would happen, so I had always skipped over reading that part of the agreement. Acting was my life, and I didn't know what this situation was going to do to my career... or if I would even have one after it was all said and done.

Aaron turned down a long drive and clicked a button to open the large black iron gate. Neal and Aaron had surprised Daisy with a new house in Los Angeles a month ago. Her men had been worried Aaron's house wasn't safe enough after she had been kidnapped again a short few months ago. They'd had the house alarmed and cameras installed everywhere. Daisy told me they'd done the same thing in her home in Ft Lauderdale. The extra security seemed to make Daisy more relaxed. She also wore a diamond necklace that contained a tracker. She had asked for the tracker after her first kidnapping.

The SUV came to a stop in front of the modern, stylish mansion. I was used to seeing large houses and being around celebrities, but Daisy's house put most of my other friends' homes to shame. John held the door open for me to get out. I was still dressed in the blue scrubs from earlier. When I glanced at my hands, I could see specks of blood under my nails.

Next to the doorbell was a screen mounted to the house. At first glance, I didn't think anything of it until Neal pressed his hand to a black screen and the door lock clicked open. John placed his hand on my lower back. His warm presence gave me a sense of security. When he moved away, I felt the loss.

Brock and Jessica were already at the house, and we all quickly settled into the living room. John poured me a drink to calm my nerves.

"What happened?" Brock asked. "We need to know so we can help you."

I nodded as I sucked down the amber liquid that burned all the way down to my stomach. "We made plans earlier in the day for him to come home after work. We were going to finish the last couple of details on the wedding and then look at our 23andMe reports. He was excited when he called and said he couldn't wait to show me mine. Nate wouldn't tell me what it said—he wanted to show me." I took a deep breath and held out my glass for more liquor. John's pour was smaller the second time, probably so they could get the story from me before I was drunk. I took another sip, smaller this time, before continuing. "When he didn't come home right away, I grabbed a glass of wine and finished the wedding details myself. When he did get home, I knew from the goofy look on his face and the smell of strange cologne on him that he'd been with his lover."

Their brows rose.

"He's gay," I explained. "I agreed to be his wife because his family would cut him off and not let him practice in the law firm anymore if he lived as openly gay."

"Why didn't he just open his own law firm?" Neal asked. "Is his parents' money that important?" He had been on his computer since we'd walked into the house. His fingers hovered over the keyboard, waiting for my answer.

I closed my eyes and remembered the first time Nate had come to my house with a broken arm and a black eye. "He tried to leave the family business multiple times. Each time was followed by me taking him to the hospital with a broken bone. One night after I came home from filming, I found Nate curled up on my couch. He was minutes away from dying. Someone had dropped him off at my house and deleted the footage as they left. Nate wouldn't tell me who it was or what was going on. He just needed a wife."

Nate and I hadn't talked often about what had happened. He would clam up and tell me not to worry about it.

"I've never had much luck in the dating realm, and we always joked that if we weren't married by the time we hit our thirties, we would marry each other. We talked about all the wedding plans together. We shared everything going on in our lives. He was one of my best friends... I mean *is*. That's why getting married wasn't such a stretch." I shrugged. "Only Nate had grown more secretive in recent days. I chalked it up to nerves over getting married. I knew that deciding to go through with it and asking me to be his fake fiancé had created a lot of stress and strife for both of us."

I took another sip. "I know he was seeing someone on the side, and I was willing to break the marriage off. But if he felt it was imperative for him to live life under the guise of being straight and keeping his boyfriend a secret, then who was I to argue? Not only did he agree to give me a very generous allowance for marrying him, but he also promised me the option to have lovers on the side, as long as I kept it quiet like he did. This all seemed more than fair. And because I love planning a party more than almost anything, I was happy to follow through with my part of the bargain."

"She does throw amazing parties," Daisy agreed.

I continued to tell the story of how I'd ended up in jail. The night before, instead of Nate indulging my whims and helping me select hors d'oeuvres and wine pairings, he had broken down and cried. The very last thing I needed was to feel like the bad guy, as if the wedding were my idea and I was the one ruining his life. That was when I'd snapped. I accused him of being ungrateful. I reminded him of everything I was giving up to help him. And I suggested that the very least he could do was to show a little gratitude and not try to make the entire experience miserable. Then I stormed off because if I'd learned anything in dealing with men, it was that having a mini-meltdown went a long way toward ensuring I would get what I wanted.

When I came home the next day from work, Nate was nowhere to be seen. He hadn't called, which was unusual for him and only served to make me feel worse about the situation. We were off to a lousy start. If I wanted to be miserable while I was married, then I could marry a straight guy. At least then I wouldn't have to go looking for sex since I would have someone who was there, ready, and on demand.

I went on to tell everyone about how I'd searched the house to find Nate. He didn't come out when I called. He didn't peek out when I slammed the door. It was highly unusual for him not to respond. I went out to the pool, which was one of his favorite spots for thinking and moping, but he wasn't there. So I headed upstairs, and that was when I spotted blood outside his bedroom. When I went in, I found blood everywhere in the bathroom. He was extremely picky, so I'd started to clean up the mess.

"That's when I picked up the knife to take it downstairs." But when I turned, I found a deputy in the doorway.

"Wait," Brock demanded. "How did the deputy find his way into your house?"

I took the last sip of the amber liquor, and the burn felt good down my throat. "That was my question to him, but he didn't like the knife in my hand. When I stepped forward, he pulled his gun. I fell and that's how I ended up covered in blood. When we finally made it downstairs is when I got my answer. Our cleaning lady called the cops because she saw blood and me walking around it."

"What is her name?" Neal asked, not looking up from his laptop.

"It's Ms. Orchard. What's even stranger is she was in our house the night before and recorded my fight with Nate. We have strict contracts with the help. No videoing in our house. She turned over the video to the police. It shows me yelling at Nate, throwing my wine on him, and storming out of the room."

John poured a little more amber liquor into my cup.

Brock clicked his phone on. "Do you have a lawyer? You shouldn't have talked to the cops without one."

I was angry, distraught, outraged, and anxious. I hadn't called my lawyer. "I didn't think I needed one. Then suddenly, they were taking me to the station to collect evidence."

John stood and started to pace back and forth in front of the tall white fireplace. "This doesn't make sense. You had a fight, and someone happened to be in your house to videotape it. Then the police show up right when you're walking around the crime scene. If they just wanted your evidence, they could've collected it there."

"They needed an official statement."

He stopped pacing and focused his gray eyes on me, causing my heart rate to increase. I didn't know why, all of a sudden, I was melting into a puddle when some man looked at me. I'd given up on finding a man that made my heart beat faster, my palms sweat, and images of dirty things pop into my mind.

"But you said they took you down to the station," he said. "You could've gone the next day to give your statement. This all sounds fucked up."

I had no clue what happened when someone went missing. "The sheriff said Nate's dad is a friend of the family and called him when Nate didn't show up to work. What I don't understand is why he thought that was such a big deal. Nate sometimes just doesn't show up for a few days."

Brock tapped his finger on his glass of amber liquor. "Do you know his family well? Could they be setting you up for his murder? You mentioned earlier he would come home beaten sometimes. Maybe it went too far this time, and they're trying to take you down."

Neal let out a whistle. "You might be onto something, Brock. Annabella, did you read Nate's will?"

Over the past week, Nate had given me lots of documents to sign before the wedding. I'd just assumed it was the prenup we had talked about. I hadn't minded signing it—Nate was worth way more than me. We'd discussed in full what it was, so when Nate had handed it to me, I'd signed without reading. "No. I know I should've, but I didn't. Someone mentioned earlier that he'd changed it, and that's another reason I'm the prime suspect."

John leveled a heated look at me. "You signed a legal document without reading it?"

I downed the amber liquor in my cup. The alcohol was starting to hit my bloodstream. It was helping keep my nerves under control. I didn't like having to explain my life to so many people. And on top of that, one of my closest friends was still missing. "Nate is my primary lawyer and has been since he graduated. He never did anything wrong before, so yes, I signed without reading. Neal, how bad is it?"

Brock leaned over Neal's shoulder. His eyes were large with surprise. "Nate's grandparents opened up the law firm. When they passed, the firm was willed to Nate, not his parents. And Nate didn't have you sign a prenup. It was his will. He changed his will last week. In case he died, you got everything. But if something happens to you, his sister will get everything."

Why would he put me in the middle of his family issues? "If he owned the firm, why did his parents have so much over him? Why not make peace? This doesn't make sense. I saw the broken arms and bruises. Someone hurt him, and now he might be dead. And I'm in charge of the fucked-up family's fortune."

I was furious. I was desperate. I no longer trusted the system. I didn't understand how I could even be in trouble. It made no sense. They had no body. "How are they making me surrender my passport if there is no body."

I was convinced Nate had injured himself or someone close to him had injured him, but deep down, I knew he was still alive. I kept waiting for him to show up with a bandage and an apology.

"Hell, I'm supposed to be on set first thing in the morning. The cops wouldn't let me take my phone. They told me it was evidence. All they did was treat me like I killed Nate, and they don't have any evidence that he's even dead. I keep thinking he's going to walk through the door at any second and think this is a funny joke. I have no credit cards on me. Everything I have is at Nate's house. I've already sold mine. Where am I supposed to go?" Tears streamed down my face.

Daisy came over and wrapped me in a hug. "You stay here tonight. We will figure everything out in the morning. I think the boys have enough to go on for a while. Let's get you settled into the guest room."

John, Aaron, and Brock were huddled around Neal as Daisy walked me out of the room. I hoped they would find something to clear my name. More than anything, I hoped my friend wasn't dead.

4

JOHN

I watched as Annabella's perky ass walked out the door. "She didn't do it." I wasn't sure if I said the words to reassure myself or my friends. My phone hadn't stopped vibrating in my pocket since I walked Annabella out of the sheriff's office. I knew it was my sister. She would want to help. But we had enough help at the moment.

Brock raised a brow. "We know, man, but it looks like someone framed her. And who knows if Nate is even dead?"

Neal pulled up the cleaning lady's picture.

"How did you pull up the photo so fast? All Annabella gave you was a last name." I pulled the screen closer to get a better look.

"I hacked into Nate's files at work the second we got here. Her contract was on his hard drive. It listed her date of birth and Social Security number. She doesn't look like someone who would frame Annabella for murder." Neal said.

I gulped down the expensive scotch, "Money. If someone paid her enough, she would do anything. Hell, Annabella said Nate would come home bruised. If someone did something to Ms. Orchard's family, she could've helped frame Anna." Brock arched his brow at the nickname I gave Annabella. I ignored him and continued. "We need to look into the cleaning lady's finances."

"Already have. Nothing. No large deposits, no extra spending. She worked for her last employer for twenty years until he died a few weeks ago. That's when Nate hired her. Nothing seemed out of the ordinary."

I looked down at Neal's laptop and the information in front of him. "But why would she go out of her way to record that conversation last night? She just happened to return to the house when Nate and Anna were having a fight and thought to record it? I don't have a housekeeper, but is it not worrisome she just walks into the house?"

Aaron spoke up for the first time. "I grew up with staff around the house. Normally, they come and go and don't announce themselves when they arrive. So her walking in is not unusual. Now the videotaping of her employers is strange. We need to talk to her.

Annabella mentioned earlier that she fired Ms. Orchard and the lady was distraught."

Brock nodded. "I'll talk to her tomorrow. Our plane is scheduled to leave tomorrow afternoon. I have a meeting with the governor. He didn't say what it was about, but I need to head back to Ft. Lauderdale tomorrow night. John, you can stay here and help Annabella out."

I had no plans to leave. I was just glad I didn't have to fight Brock about it. "Did Anna mention who Nate was dating? We should talk to him to see if he knows more than she does. The way she made it sound, Nate had been with the same man for a while. If he loved this man, why did he give everything to Anna? Could his lover have been the one to kill him or make it look like he's dead to set up Anna?"

The more I thought about the case, the more I realized how much Nate's will caused a bigger issue. Anna would go from a millionaire to a billionaire if he was really dead. She would have everyone coming at her in all directions if we couldn't find more information about what was going on.

"So we're all in agreement that she's innocent?" I asked, needing reassurance from my friends.

Neal looked up from his laptop. "She may be a tad superficial and seriously jaded, but she's also utterly lacking in devious ways. She's quick to anger, but not malicious in the least. I have some searches running, and I reached out to a few people online to gain more information. Let's start back up in the morning and see if we can come up with a game plan.

Brock and Jessica headed for the guesthouse. Neal and Aaron headed for the master bedroom. I walked down the hall of guest rooms toward mine but stopped when I was outside of Anna's. My fingers itched to knock on the door and demand more answers. Instead, I slid down the wall outside her door and pulled out the notebook with the list of information.

I'd learned that leaving an electronic trail could be incredibly damaging, so I always had pens and paper at my disposal. My notes on the case were too important to trust to the police. They figured they already had their killer. Sure, Anna had the financial motives, to an extent, but she was no slouch when it came to earning money or being financially stable. She had her own money.

I had to know a few things. I listed out my questions. She had laid out her recollections of the night, but I needed to ask about more significant issues, starting with a lot of whys. No matter how many ways I looked at the evidence, it appeared obvious that someone was trying to set her up. I wanted to sweep her up into my arms and take her away from everything. But I had to face reality. We needed to figure out who was trying to frame her and what had happened to Nate.

I finally drifted off to sleep, sitting against the wall outside her room, once I was convinced the place was safe and so was Annabella.

ANNABELLA

When I walked out in the morning and saw John sitting by my door, I jumped and clutched my chest while he looked away and tried to hide a frown. "Sorry. Didn't expect to find anyone outside my door," I mumbled.

The way he was hiding his face, I knew what he thought. Obviously, he was convinced it was the sight of him that had me off balance. But the sight of him made my body hum. Last night, I had tossed and turned in bed—not because I might be convicted of murder, but because images of John had kept circling through my mind. The way he'd walked into the sheriff's station with purpose and meaning. The scar on the side of his face that he kept trying to hide was sexy as hell. I wanted to run my hand down his face. Well, that wasn't the only place I wanted to run my hands. Closing my eyes, I tried to get my body back under control.

"Wanna get some coffee with me?" I asked. I felt awkward. I normally had a strict schedule, but after being arrested, my schedule had suddenly cleared. I'd canceled everything that hadn't already been canceled. Last night, I'd used Daisy's phone to contact my manager, who was in hysterics by the time I talked to him. It had taken me an hour to calm him down, and he'd agreed to cancel all of my future engagements until further notice. In two days, I was scheduled to make an appearance at a local art show. I wasn't even sure why I was scheduled for the art show other than my manager said it would be good press. The director of *Last Love* had put my scheduling on hold and was shooting everything else. The studio didn't plan to cut my section out of the movie... yet. He hadn't said those words, but I knew they were there between us.

I sighed. "I'm free. Sort of."

He smirked, and that little twitch of his lips made him even sexier. We made our way down to the kitchen together. We weren't the only ones who were awake at such an early hour.

Brock was up, and Daisy was sitting with him. "You're awake," she noted quietly.

I nodded. "Yes. And I wish I weren't. I can't handle turning on the television, the news, and social media." I rubbed my face. "Everyone thinks I'm some kind of scorned lover turned killer."

"I don't," John mumbled.

I snickered. "I have a small cheering section." I reached out and patted his hand. "Thank you for that."

He quickly left the table, his face turning several shades of pink, and went to make the coffees.

All of my emotions were so close to the surface, I was afraid they might erupt at any moment. "What do we do next?" I asked. "Nate hasn't magically appeared overnight? I really need to get my phone back."

Daisy and Brock exchanged a look. "No. He hasn't."

I groaned. "I don't understand. What could've happened?"

"We need to get back in the house and look around as soon as they release the crime scene," Brock said. "In the meantime, you need to collect all the assets that you can. Just in case." He nodded at John, who was returning to the table with mugs of coffee.

"I didn't know how you liked it," he mumbled as he set a mug down in front of me then pushed the cream and sugar toward me.

"I don't suppose you have any Baileys?" I asked. His lips twitched. "Kahlúa?"

He sank down in the empty seat beside me. "I'm pretty sure you need to be on top of your game right now. You can't be drinking." He glanced at Brock, who nodded.

"When this is all over, mimosas on the beach," Daisy promised. "You pick the beach."

My eyes watered. "Thank you. Greece maybe. Or we could go to some beach in Mexico." I rubbed my eyes.

"First, let's clear your name and find out what's going on with Nate," Brock urged. "Have you been too Nate's office before?"

"Yes, many times. When we were kids, we spent hours at the firm, and I would stop over every so often in the last few years."

"Good. Can you get John into his office?" When I nodded, Brock continued. "John, look around to see if you find anything and put this into the computer." Brock handed John a thumb drive. "This will give me access to Nate's computer and the network. Jessica and I need to leave around six tonight."

My heart sank as I wondered what would happen if we didn't find out what was going on by six.

John squeezed my shoulder. "I'm going to stay until we figure out what is happening." I let out the breath I didn't know I was holding. "Antonio and Kat are also here to help if we need them."

Daisy smirked. "You only need Kat if you need to take someone out. And she's a long way from her alligators, so we would need to find her acid to get rid of the bodies." she said with the straightest face.

"Alligators?"

John rolled his eyes. "Kat has a slight issue with killing people and feeding them to alligators. Antonio said she hasn't killed anyone in the past month."

Daisy burst out laughing. "So Antonio thinks. I'm

pretty sure I saw a large black bag of something in her SUV the other day."

I looked back and forth among them, trying to figure out if they were serious. "Um, are we going to need to kill anyone? I'm trying to prove my innocence, not kill someone."

John took a sip of his coffee. "Don't worry about it. We won't need to kill anyone."

"When do you think I can get my phone back? Nate and I set up Find My Friends. We only use it when we really need to. That might tell us where he is." I hadn't thought of that earlier.

Neal shook his head. "I hacked your account last night and looked. His last location was the house before he left. It's like he turned his phone off when he left. Did he ever tell you the name of the person he was sleeping with?"

"Pedro. They've been together for the past three years."

John tapped his fingers on the table. "See, that is what I don't understand. Why would he turn everything over to you and give nothing to a man he spent three years with?"

"Because he never wanted his family to know who his lover was. I promised to take care of Pedro financially if anything happened to Nate. I met him a few times over the years. They truly loved each other."

Brock got up and poured another cup of coffee.

"Maybe Pedro killed him and made it look like you did it. They could've gotten into a fight. Hell, if I were him, I would be upset with him marrying someone else."

A shiver ran down my spine. "Would Pedro frame me? No. There's something else going on. I need my phone and access to the house safe."

John squeezed my shoulder again. "Why don't you go get ready?"

I ran upstairs, showered, and dressed in an outfit that Daisy had laid out for me. The only clothing I had at the moment were the blue scrubs the police had given me to change into. I didn't care if I never saw those again. My memories of blue scrubs would be forever tied to the jail.

5

ANNABELLA

Our first stop was Nate's office. Security surrounded me the second we walked into the skyscraper downtown. The building displayed Nate's family's name. They weren't only rich, but they had one of the most well-known names in Los Angeles. Jake, the head of security, immediately blocked my path as we walked through the door. He had been one of the family's top guards for the past five years. Now he stood between me and answers.

John stepped in front of me and addressed Jake before he had the chance to speak. "She's not convicted. Back off. She has every right to be here. According to the will, if Nate is dead, she owns this place."

The guy glared, but I continued on, all the while struggling to hold my head up.

"You can be sad," John murmured as the elevator door closed. "It might look better if you were."

I glared at him while he pushed the button for the seventy-second floor. "Are you trying to tell me what to feel?"

He chuckled. "Maybe. You're an actress. Think of me as your director. I'm just telling you that these people may be called to testify against you. Give them something nice to say. Look devastated. Pretend you lost your future husband. He was murdered. Sudden. Scary. And all your money might get tied up." He shook his head before the doors opened on the top floor of the office building. "I don't know why people tie themselves to others, but whatever."

He laid a hand on my lower back as he guided me out of the elevator. Everyone was staring at us. I'd expected as much. I walked past reception and continued down the long hallway to Nate's office. I didn't need to hear the footsteps behind me to know John was on my trail. A few doors opened behind us, and I felt more stares as we walked by. With each step, my bravado started to fade. It was easier to act, knowing everything was fake. This wasn't fake, and I was furious at Nate for putting me in such an uncomfortable position. When I reached the waiting room for his office, I found Sidney, his assistant, sitting at her desk with a box of tissues.

"I'm trying to collect some items of sentimental

value," I explained when she got up from her desk. When she opened her mouth to speak, I kept talking. "This isn't a crime scene. And not that you care, but I didn't do it."

The assistant muttered something under her breath about how Nate never loved me.

I froze. "What makes you say that?"

Sidney was quiet, but I sensed there was more to her comment.

"You know, I was supposed to be his beard," I said, not that it was any of her business. "We're old friends. I was tired of men using me for my money. Nate was tired of people questioning his sexual orientation and dealing with his family."

I watched the girl for a reaction. She looked back down the hall toward Nate's father's office. His sister Elizabeth also had an office in the building. I planned to stop by and find out what she knew about the will.

"Still, he was always discreet," I continued. "And I was fine with that. Except now he's missing, and I'm the suspect. Do you know much about who he was seeing?"

The girl sat down behind her desk. She looked uncomfortable. The girl tapped her finger on her desk as a nervous gesture.

"Sidney, right?"

She nodded.

"I don't need his money. I didn't need a place to live.

We're friends. And this was convenient. Why would I do anything to jeopardize my career?" I covered my face with both hands. "How could I do anything to hurt my best friend?" I shook my head.

"Pedro," the girl whispered. "He's Italian. He came for a business meeting, and they hit it off."

I blinked a few times. "Okay, so he still sees the same man." I winked at Sidney. "Any chance you have a picture of him?" I didn't have one on me to give to John and Neal.

"Was he really reconsidering the wedding?" Sidney asked.

Deciding honesty was the best policy, I nodded. "Yes. But not for the reasons everyone thinks. He wanted to marry his lover instead. But the issues with his family held him back. I would do anything to make Nate happy. It's not like I had men lining up at my door to make me their wife." I leaned in. "Did you know he changed his will last week?"

"Yes. He admitted getting it done fast. Marta helped get everything done." Sidney sighed. "There's a picture of Pedro under your picture in the office."

"Thank you, Sidney." I grabbed a pen and Post-it from her desk and wrote down my number. "I'm apprehensive about Nate. If you hear or see anything, let me know."

Sidney looked at the pink sticky I handed her. "You really think he's okay?"

"Yes." The word came out before I had time to think about it. Was Nate hurt? Probably. But everything told me he was still alive.

John pulled the double wood doors to Nate's office open. We wandered inside the office, and John made a beeline for the desk. He found the frame with the picture. He pulled it open, and sure enough, there was a second picture behind mine. He flipped it over and found an address on the back. "This whole thing is coming with us," he announced.

I shrugged, not understanding why we needed everything.

Security would let Nate's family know I was in his office. I wouldn't be surprised if Richard, Nate's dad, burst in at any second. In the meantime, I worked on the wall safe. I opened it on the first try since I knew the combination by heart. It was the same one for all of Nate's safes. Inside, I found a copy of the will. I scanned the document. As promised, I was the one who stood to inherit everything upon Nate's death. In addition, there was one stack of hundred-dollar bills wrapped with a white-and-yellow band. Across the front the in yellow lettering, it read "ten thousand dollars." I frowned.

"What's wrong?" John asked, looking at the money.

Most people probably thought that finding ten grand was pretty good, but I knew better. "He usually kept one hundred grand or more on hand in the safe."

I went to the door and leaned out to speak with Sidney. I asked if anyone else had been there before us.

She shook her head. "No one besides Nate and Pedro were ever in the office."

I was shocked to hear Pedro had been there.

I put the stack of money into my purse just as Mr. Fisher rounded the corner, followed closely by Nate's sister. Mr. Fisher had short black hair, which was speckled with gray. He was always dressed in the most expensive suit, and he walked with power and authority. In all the years I'd known Nate, I had only seen his dad out of a suit a handful of times.

"What are you doing here, Annabella? You are not welcome," Mr. Fisher said coldly.

John shifted to my side as I spoke. "Well, I'm looking for signs of where my fiancé could be. And if something did happen to him, I have every right to be here."

He barked out a laugh. "My son went off and got himself killed this time, and you are the prime suspect. No matter what that will says, you won't get anything. Because you will be behind bars."

"Dad, Nate probably just went off on one of his trips. He's stressed about the upcoming wedding. Annabella will be your daughter in a matter of weeks."

Mr. Fisher's jaw clenched, and a bead of sweat trickled down his face. "If he would've done like I told him and grown up, we wouldn't be in this predicament." Before I could ask what he was talking about, the man turned on his heel and left.

Marta walked up and wrapped her arms around me. I pulled back after a moment. Marta sat in one of the guest chairs, and I took the one next to her. John leaned against the back wall. I didn't know how one man could look so sexy just leaning against the wall. Marta cleared her throat, and John smirked, probably because he knew I was staring.

"Sorry," I mumbled. "Do you know where Nate is? He can't be dead."

Marta leaned back in the chair. She had long blond hair and was dressed in a black suit with a crisp white shirt. Upon closer inspection, I found that her eyes were red and bloodshot. "I tried calling you last night, but your phone is going to voice mail."

John walked over and snagged two bottles of water from Nate's bar. Then he handed one to Marta and one to me. I would've rather had a sip of his expensive scotch.

"My phone is at the house, which is a crime scene," I explained. "You have to give me something. Deep down, I don't think he's dead. Something is going on, and he wouldn't tell me what. Lately, it seemed he was hiding more and more secrets from me. We used to tell each other everything."

Marta looked back toward the door. "Things are going on at the firm. Nate didn't want you tied up in it.

Let's just say Dad started doing business with the wrong crowd. Nate was working to clean it up."

"Is that who broke his arm?"

Marta's eyes widened. "No. Nate told me you were playing around and accidentally pushed him into the pool. He said he hit the side and broke his arm."

I couldn't help but grind my teeth. "Lie. He came home half dead, and I rushed him to the hospital. Does anyone know the truth? Have you met Pedro?" Nate's sister knew Nate and I were marrying to fulfill the family obligation. She shook her head. John walked over and handed her the photo of Nate's boyfriend.

Marta studied the picture for a moment. "I've seen them together a few times, but I didn't know his name. Nate and I fought about the wedding yesterday. It's bullshit you have to go through this for him. Don't get me wrong. I love you like a sister, and that's why I agreed to help him with the will."

I shook my head. "I didn't even know I was signing a will. I thought it was our prenup."

Marta cocked her head to the side. "He wasn't drawing up a prenup for you guys. I don't know where he is or if he's hurt. I just want my brother back. Father is getting anxious because Nate was working on something for a client that we're worried about."

John stepped forward. "Why not drop the client?"

"It's more complicated than that. I've said too much

already. Please find my brother. Like you, I believe he's okay."

I hugged Marta goodbye and watched as she left the office.

I glanced around Nate's office, looking for any type of clues. John was looking through all the documents on his desk but found nothing of importance. We were about to leave with more questions than answers. John rested his hand on my lower back as we walked down the hall.

We entered the waiting elevator, and when it was about to close, two men stepped in. John pulled me closer and tightened his grip around my waist. The two men spoke Italian as the elevator went down. With each word they spoke, John pulled me closer to his side. It seemed as though he understood what they said. When the doors to the elevator opened, he held me back and let the men get a few feet ahead of us. One looked back over his shoulder at us.

John had his phone to his ear. "We have a problem." He didn't wait for the person on the other end to speak. "We went to Nate's office, and when we left, Vito Costello and Dawood Bruno walked out and entered the elevator."

That time, I heard Brock cuss on the phone.

John ignored him and continued. "I'm pretty sure they didn't know I spoke Italian. For being the most feared mob boss, he didn't even try to conceal his identity. He told the man next to him to get Carmine into town. You know who he is, right?"

"No," I mumbled, not expecting John to answer me since he was talking to Brock.

But John turned to me. "Carmine is the top assassin for the mob. Nobody has seen him. They only hear about the number of people he kills.

6

JOHN

Annabella looked out the window of my SUV. She'd become extra quiet since learning we might be dealing with the mob. I asked if she wanted to go back to Daisy's and told her I would go to her house, but she stood firm and said she wanted to go to the house.

She'd seemed so untouchable when I'd watched her on TV and seen her doing charity work, but each minute I stayed around her, I learned more about her. She tried to put on a robust outer image, but she wanted someone to lean on.

I couldn't help but groan as my phone rang in my pocket again. Addie hadn't stopped trying to call.

Annabella tore her eyes away from the window and looked over at me. "Girlfriend?"

My lips twitched. It almost sounded like she was jealous. "Nope. Sister."

She arched her eyebrows, opening up her pretty green eyes even more. They reminded me of a green flower field in the spring, rich and full of wonder. "She's a little upset with me. I promised I would FaceTime her when you went to Daisy's event. Then everything happened. She's been blowing up my phone since the second I escorted you out of the sheriff's office.

Annabella held out her hand. "Give me your phone."

"You don't have to talk to my sister. You have enough on your mind."

She rolled those pretty green eyes. All I wanted to do was reach across the seat, lay her across my lap, and redden her ass. The image made my dick instantly hard and uncomfortable. I shifted in my seat and handed her my phone just when it started to ring again.

When Annabella swiped to answer, my sister's voice came across the speakers in the car.

"About time you answer your phone, big brother. I could have been abducted or needed food." Addie was always a little on the dramatic side.

"Sis, an abductor wouldn't call that many times. Also, I know you don't need food. I had food delivered to your house yesterday."

She huffed on the other end of the line. "You don't need to keep doing that. I can have my food delivered. And don't think I didn't notice it's the same man each time. How much extra do you pay him to check on me?"

Now I shifted in my seat uncomfortably, not because my dick hurt, but because Addie knew I had someone checking on her. "Hey, sis, I have someone in the car who would like to say hi."

"Hi, Ad—" Annabella didn't even get out my sister's name before Addie let out a shriek so loud, it made my ears ring. Annabella's face lit up with the biggest smile. It was the first time I had seen her smile in the past twenty-four hours, and I wanted to see her smile like that again.

"Oh my God!" Addie exclaimed. "I've seen every movie you've made—*Running from Justice, Mistaken Love, Cops on the Run, Affairs, Kept,* and I watch you when you're on TV for awards."

I laughed. "Breathe, Addie."

My sister ignored me. "And your charity work with agoraphobia is amazing. Not many people put time into that charity. You know how amazing you are for that? When does your next movie come out? What is it like working with Aaron Ross and Jake Mansfield?"

"Sis, let her answer your questions, and you've met Aaron Ross before."

She didn't stop. "Are you going to work with Jake

again? I like it when you two work together." She took a deep breath. "Also, I don't think you killed your fiancé since it's a marriage of convenience, not love. And wow, that will!"

Annabella looked at me with a raised brow.

"You need to stop hacking," I mumbled to my sister, even though I knew she wouldn't listen to me.

Addie huffed out a breath. "Like Neal and Brock didn't hack to see what they could find to help out."

"Well, you asked a lot of questions, so let's see if I can answer all of this," Annabella said kindly. "You are correct—I didn't kill Nate. Yes, I like working with Jake and Aaron. They're both charming."

"Aww," Addie cooed.

"I'm glad you like all of my movies. I'm shooting *Last Love* at the moment." Annabella paused for a second before she continued. "Agoraphobia is close to my heart. My mother had a severe case of agoraphobia and never left the house. She got really sick from cancer when I was eighteen and wouldn't go to the hospital, so she ended up dying."

I reached over, grabbed Annabella's hand, and squeezed it.

My sister was quiet for a moment. "Don't worry, John," Addie finally said. "I still go to the doctor."

Annabella's head swung in my direction. I mouthed, "She has agoraphobia."

Annabella's eyes flickered with something I didn't

understand, and she squeezed my hand. "Where do you live, Addie?"

"Boston. I own a PI firm out here."

"Next time I'm in Boston, I will bring you a cup of coffee, and we can sit down and talk about all the movies I've been in."

Addie squealed. "I can't wait for that. John will give you my number. Bye, big brother."

"Bye, pip-squeak." Before she could answer, I clicked off the phone.

"How old is your sister?"

"Thirty-five. We're the same age—she's my twin."

Annabella twisted her hands in her lap. I could tell she wanted to ask more questions.

"Our mother also had agoraphobia. I didn't notice the signs in Addie until it was too late. Our mom disappeared when we were young, and I spent so much time trying to make sure we had a house and food, I forgot to make sure my sister spent more time out. She isn't as bad as our mom. She will leave the house when she has to, but she prefers not to leave at all."

"How does she run a PI firm?"

I couldn't hold back my smile. "Never wanting to leave the house, Addie spent hours on the computer. She codes and learned to hack. Brock uses her sometimes when we have too many cases. All of her employees do the fieldwork and report back to her."

"I'm glad she can make it work. Do you mind me

asking how your mother disappeared when she has agoraphobia?"

I parked the SUV in Annabella's front yard, behind a squad car. "That's the reason Addie opened her firm. She doesn't think my mom wandered off. She thinks someone took her. I don't know why they would've. She never left the house. But Addie won't drop the case. She continues to look for our mom."

"I hope she finds your mom." Annabella's eyes shifted from me to the squad car. "Why are the cops still here?"

"They're probably still collecting evidence."

Annabella let out a frustrated sigh next to me. Her hands were clenched into fists. "I just want to get things out of my house." She threw the passenger door open and stomped up the driveway to her house.

I held back the smile I wanted to release. Annabella was a spitfire and had a temper. I jogged the couple of steps to catch up to her. We didn't need her getting arrested for yelling or assaulting a cop.

An officer stood at the doorway with his arms crossed.

"I want to go into my house," she said firmly.

"We're still processing the home, ma'am."

Annabella rolled her eyes. "Really? Ma'am? You know who I am. I don't care if you follow me to make sure I don't touch anything I'm not allowed to. But I want into my house to get clothes."

An older officer walked over. "Let her in." When the younger man started to protest, the older gentleman held up a hand. "We're packing up to leave. The house is no longer a crime scene."

Annabella pushed past the younger officer and walked toward the stairs. I followed her as she passed a bedroom with crime tape and headed farther down the hall.

"Where are you going?"

She glanced over her shoulder. "My room." I must have looked confused because she explained. "We don't sleep in the same room. I told you last night I was his beard. Nate is gay. We never shared a bed and never will share a bed." She shrugged. "I may need money for my defense since Brock told me mine and Nate's accounts are frozen. I plan to take what money we have here in the safe."

Even though the police said they were leaving, an officer followed us into the bedroom. I wanted to tell him to go, but that might make it look like we were hiding something. Annabella grabbed a pink roller bag from the closet and started throwing clothes into the bag.

The officer standing in the doorway cleared his throat. "Why do you need a bag if we cleared the house?"

Annabella stopped packing and looked at me. "He's right. I can stay here."

I shook my head fervently. "You are not staying here. We don't know if someone tried to kill Nate. What happens if they come back for you? It's not safe." I turned toward the officer. "And you should know that more than anyone. Do you have any leads?"

He didn't say anything but just continued to write as Annabella packed her bag. Her eyes were trained on the suitcase.

I walked over to her. "Keep packing, and we will get back to Daisy's."

"Am I putting them in danger? I don't want anything to happen to Daisy. She's already been through so much."

I reached up and wiped a tear from Annabella's cheek. "Nothing is going to happen to you or Daisy, but staying here is not safe. We don't know what happened, and we need to talk about everything with Brock."

Annabella nodded and continued to pack. She went into the bathroom to grab a couple more items. Once she had her clothes packed, I picked up the bag and followed her down the hall. She stopped at the doorway to Nate's room and took a deep breath before walking in. I noticed bloody footprints on the white carpet.

Annabella walked toward the closet and moved the small dresser next to it to reveal a floor safe. She spun the dials on it a couple times before I heard the safe click open. She opened it with no problem, which should've helped ease the mind of the officer. He stood at the door, watching everything she did. We all leaned over the floor safe, and Annabella frowned.

"The money is essentially gone." She shook her head and pulled out one single stack. Nate had left a note on it for her. "Emergency money, darling. You know, like you just have to have that Prada purse." He'd signed it with a winky face.

Annabella put the money in her purse.

"You can't take that," the officer said.

I stood up and blocked his path. "I've let you follow us around like a lost dog, but the officer downstairs said the house had been cleared. I don't know why you're here. She hasn't been charged with anything, and this is her house."

The officer stepped back and crossed his arms. He looked like he wanted to say something. Instead, he nodded and left the room.

I reached out my hand and helped Annabella get up off the floor.

"Why do the cops seem to have an issue with me?" she asked.

"That's a good question. You did say earlier that Nate's dad is friends with the sheriff. Let's get your stuff and go. Do you have everything?"

"Almost. I want to grab my scripts and jewelry out of the study safe."

I followed her down the stairs and looked out the window. The police were gone.

"I have some scripts in there. I'm supposed to be reading them." She swallowed hard. "In case anyone still wants to work with me."

I followed her into the study and stopped at the desk to look through some paperwork. Anything would help with the case. I grabbed the laptop off the desk. I would bring it back to the house for Neal to look at.

"There should also be more money in this safe along with my jewelry." Annabella took a Monet off the wall and opened the safe behind it. Her jewelry wasn't there either. She frowned. "I bought that jewelry. Could Nate have been having money issues?"

"We'll have Neal look into his financials, but I assume he would have already found that yesterday when he was looking into Nate."

The more we looked into Nate's life, the more I thought he was on the run, especially with two house safes empty except for one stack of bills.

A loud crashing sound came from the kitchen. We weren't alone in the house.

7

ANNABELLA

John shoved me behind him and grabbed his gun. I didn't even know he had a gun on him. "Stay," he barked as he walked out the door of the study.

I had never been good at listening to orders, which was probably why I was marrying a man as a favor instead of dealing with men that I might be able to have a relationship with. I grabbed the scissors off of Nate's desk and went through the door John had just walked through.

The moment my heel clicked against the hardwood floor, John looked over his shoulder and glared at me. Damn, that man was even sexy when he was mad. I slipped out of my heels and padded behind him. When he entered the kitchen, I heard a loud scream.

Rounding the corner, I ran into a hard body. John had stopped a few feet into the chef's kitchen.

I peeked around his massive body and found my ex-housekeeper trying to enter the security room.

"What are you doing here?" I yelled. "I could have you arrested for breaking and entering."

The older lady had her hands up, but she still glared in my direction. "I came to get a few of my things."

"John, put the gun down."

He held the gun pointed directly at Ms. Orchard for several long moments before he finally lowered it.

"So you thought you would enter my home and get what you need?" I asked her. "That is not how it works. You were fired. On top of that, you broke an NDA when you recorded my fiancé and me." When I said fiancé, John tensed beside me.

The older lady sat down on a barstool. "Why do you keep acting like you don't know? You're behind this. They told me you were." Tears streamed down her face.

John looked at me for answers, but I didn't have any.

"Who?" I asked, confused.

She sniffled a few times before answering. "I don't know who they are. All I know is I have to do everything they want or they're going to hurt my son."

The hair stood up on the back of my neck. I

grabbed a soda from the fridge and took the seat next to her. "Ms. Orchard, what is your son's name?"

John didn't sit down. Instead, he leaned his hip against the counter and watched the woman like a hawk. He crossed his arms, causing his black T-shirt to stretch tightly over his bulging biceps. He seemed to work hard to always angle himself so the scar on the side of his face was turned away.

"Pedro Orchard," she whispered.

I hoped the surprise didn't show on my face. "Did you know your son was dating my fiancé?"

Ms. Orchard's eyes darted back to the security room. "Yes."

"Is that why you framed me for Nate's supposed murder?"

"But they *are* missing. The men who have been after Nate and Pedro told me you're working with them as well."

"I'm not working with anyone who would hurt Nate. He's my best friend, and I would do anything for him, hence the marriage to a man who is only my friend." I pushed my soda away. I needed something stronger. The whiskey John had given me the other night would taste good right then.

John leaned forward, his eyes intense on Ms. Orchard. "What did they want you to do with the tape?"

The older woman blushed, but she didn't answer.

"The police would've grabbed the video footage," I said. "Why would anyone think the footage was still here?"

Ms. Orchard sniffled. "I wanted to look to see if there was something unusual. My boy is missing, and I'm worried."

Nate had been keeping so many secrets from me—hiring his boyfriend's mother to be our housekeeper. Every time more evidence came to light, it made me question our friendship. I'd planned to marry Nate because I didn't think he would hurt me like men had in the past, but apparently I was wrong.

"Is there anything else you can tell us?" John asked. "When did your son go missing?"

"The same night Nate did. I went to Pedro's house earlier that morning, and his place was turned upside down. When I went to leave, I was approached by two men. They told me if I wanted to see my son again, I needed to go to Nate's house and call the cops once you arrived. So I called the cops. I figured since they knew your name, you were behind this."

"If I was in on it, why would I want you to call the cops on me?"

Ms. Orchard's mouth opened a couple of times as confusion washed over her. "I didn't think that much about it. I just want my boy back." She wept into her hands.

John reached over and held her hand. I wasn't

happy she'd broken into my house. I understood she wanted her son back. I wanted my life back. And I really wanted to have a long conversation with my best friend... maybe soon-to-be-ex-best friend. Not only was I suspected for a murder, but he'd taken my jewelry. One of the pieces was my mother's.

John patted Ms. Orchard's hand. "How about you come with us? We can help you find your son."

Wait. What? "I think we should talk about this."

John leveled his gray eyes on me. "Ms. Orchard might be able to help us put things together faster. Also, someone is working to keep something quiet. Let's get back to Daisy's house and talk with the team."

NEAL, Aaron, and John sat around Daisy's dining room table, asking Ms. Orchard questions. Daisy walked up beside me and handed me a glass of wine. "You seem more upset than when you left this morning."

I let out the sigh I had been holding. "She called the cops on me. She's also the mother of my fiancé's lover. He hired her and didn't tell me their connection. Nate and I used to be so close, and over the last couple of months, all he's done is lie to me and hide things." I reached into the fridge and pulled out cold cuts and cheese. It was close to dinnertime, and my stomach had started to growl.

Daisy grabbed the bread and set it on the counter. She played with the edge of the bag for a few seconds. "If you find Nate, are you going to go through with the wedding?"

Am I? The answer seemed fairly clear. "No. I agreed to marry Nate to help him. What he did these past few days is uncalled for. The evidence might look like he's dead, but I know something isn't right. He cleared out all the money from the safes and took my jewelry. Most of it I didn't care about, but the necklace from my mom was all I had of her."

Daisy frowned as she pulled out the bread and laid a few pieces on a plate. "I only met Nate a few times. But he's a grown man and needs to stand up for himself. You can't keep being someone for him to lean on."

I reached into the silverware drawer and grabbed a butter knife then started smearing mayo across the bread. "You're right. I'm going to find him, prove my innocence, and move on." My eyes darted to the sexy man sitting at the table. He didn't seem to care what movies I was in or how much money I had.

"Um, Daisy, is John like Neal and Aaron?"

"Bisexual?"

"No," I whispered. "Is he into the other stuff?"

Daisy reached up and ran her fingers along her necklace. "Yes." She shifted her feet. "He took care of me for a few years after they rescued me."

Jealousy clouded my vision.

"But we never slept together. Don't get me wrong—he's slept with many women at Club Sanctorum. You like him, don't you?"

"Yes. But too much is going on around me to weed through my feelings for John." I grabbed the sandwich tray and walked toward the table, wondering what it would be like to have John run his hands down my body. If I didn't think about that, the only thing I would think about was the fact that my best friend was missing. The seat next to John was empty. I placed the tray of sandwiches on the table and took the chair next to him.

He was looking at the photo of Nate and Pedro that we'd taken from Nate's office. "We need to go here," John murmured. Then he pulled the picture out of the frame. "We need to check out the address. Was it a vacation spot, or is this where Pedro lives?"

Pedro's mother traced the photo. "They went on vacation there last year."

The sound of my phone ringing stopped all conversation. I snatched my phone out of my pocket, and my lawyer's name flashed across the screen. With Nate being in the wind, I'd hired an attorney my manager had told me about in the past.

"Hello," I answered.

"Ms. Harper, this is Marty. I just spoke with the judge handling your case. They feel you're a flight risk and want you to bring in your passport. They set a date for you to appear in court. The DA doesn't want a circus. There was talk of a plea deal."

"Plea deal for what? There is no body, and Nate has only been gone for one day. Why aren't they spending time finding him instead of trying to frame me for murder? The sheriff said I had forty-eight hours to bring it in."

John reached over and squeezed my thigh.

"Ms. Harper, there is evidence against you. The sheriff wants you to come in today. I think you should hear the plea deal out."

"I didn't kill anyone," I yelled into the phone. This was ridiculous. I clicked off the phone and hung up.

"You need a new lawyer," John urged. "There's no body. There can be no plea deal. Don't even think about it."

I shook my head. "I'm not. I'm thinking about running. I want to get the hell out of here. I just want to disappear for a while. This makes no sense, and you're right." I sighed. "The police are out to convict me."

"Found it," Neal mumbled between bites of his sandwich. We were all seated in the dining room of Daisy's house. Neal had overtaken the table and turned it into a war room.

Everyone crowded around the computer. He had a satellite image of a private mansion. The feed was live. There were people there, but it was impossible to tell who. The television crime shows exaggerated the abilities of those types of programs. If this were *CSI*, they would have found the killer already.

I rubbed my hand down my face. "So let's go."

John squeezed my shoulder. "You just had your passport revoked. We need to take it in."

"Can we run before I have to turn it in? I want to go now and figure out what is happening. If that is Nate there, he has a lot of explaining to do, and I'm not waiting for him to come back here to explain."

Neal twisted in his seat. "Do you really want to go?"

"No," John barked. "It could be dangerous."

"If you go with her, it might not be as bad," Neal said. "You could go by boat and be there in about a week."

"Fine. We go by boat. When can we go?" I asked the room.

John ran his hand through his shoulder-length hair. He didn't have it up in its standard ponytail. "Have you ever stayed in a small boat for days? There are no maid services or house cleaners. It would be me, you, and a boat captain. There might be rough water. And once we get to Nicaragua, we would need to stay under the radar. This means being dropped off and swimming to shore, walking through the woods, and staying in a cabin off the beaten path."

I didn't care what I had to go through. "I'm going."

John looked at everyone else in the room for

backup, but nobody answered or said a word. Neal shrugged and smirked like he knew something we didn't.

"Fine," John finally said. "We leave tomorrow night." He got up, grabbed his phone, and stormed out of the kitchen.

8

JOHN

The dark coffee tasted good. I sat the cup down on the kitchen counter in Daisy's house. I still couldn't believe I was traveling to another country with Anna. I recalculated the mileage using an online nautical map program. From Los Angeles to Nicaragua, it was 2,400 miles. Even with the two men we'd hired to sail the boat nonstop, the trip would take three days. I ran my hand through my wet hair and pulled it back into a band. I was going to be spending three days in tight quarters with one of the most beautiful women I'd ever seen. And she was engaged.

My phone vibrated on the counter. Gabriel's name flashed across the screen. He was one of the new hires Brock had brought on last week. He was a quiet guy, and I hadn't talked to him much.

"Gabriel," I answered.

"Boat's loaded and ready to go, boss.

"I'm not your boss."

Gabriel barked out a laugh. "Okay, sir. Jacob just brought in the last of the groceries. What time do you plan to leave?"

I took another sip of my dark coffee. "We leave at sundown."

"You think bringing the girl along is the best idea?"

I wanted to scream *No!* I'd spent an hour on the phone with Brock the night before, talking about my concerns. But for some reason, the man had lost his fucking mind and thought that Annabella leaving town was the best idea in case someone was after her.

"It doesn't matter. Brock set this all in motion. I'm going to drop her passport off this morning. Neal found someone locally for us to use to get her a change of identification."

Annabella's face had been all over the news for the past couple of days. Top Movie Star Suspected in Killing Her Fiancé. Every picture that had been taken of her in the past ten years was being analyzed as people tried to figure out if she was capable of murder.

"Okay. See you tonight, boss." Fucker hung up the phone before I could say anything.

I took the last sip of my coffee when Aaron walked into the kitchen. He grabbed a cup out of the cupboard and poured himself some coffee. "That tastes like shit," Aaron grumbled before pouring his down the drain.

"I made it on the lighter side." I glanced at the clock and saw that it was six in the morning. "What are you doing up so early?"

Aaron took the pot of coffee and poured what was left into my cup before preparing another pot. "Daisy woke up from a nightmare. She and Neal are showering. I came down to make coffee and breakfast. Why are you up?"

"Too much on my mind. Is Daisy still seeing a psychiatrist?"

He pulled out eggs and bacon from the fridge. "She talks to her psychiatrist each week and does video calls when she's out here. It breaks my heart when she wakes up screaming. In the past few months, she's told me stories about what happened. I wish I could go back in time and kill the fucker."

I shifted in my seat. The day we rescued Daisy came to mind. The dungeon her captor had held her in in his basement was nothing like a BDSM club. Torture chamber was a more accurate description.

"I still can't believe Brock is letting Annabella come look for Nate," I told Aaron.

Annabella stormed into the kitchen and placed her hands on her hips. "*Let* me? What day and age are we living in? I have every right to be a part of this."

I sighed. "We don't know what we're getting into.

And on top of that, if I went alone, I could fly down, check out what's going on, and be back within a day."

"This is my life. You can do whatever you want, but I plan to find Nate."

Aaron rested his hip against the counter and watched Annabella and I talk back and forth. He wore a smirk across his face.

I could feel my jaw tense. "Do you not understand how dangerous this is? When we left Nate's office yesterday, we saw two mob employees. On top of that, Pedro's mom was threatened, and the police want to make an example out of you."

Annabella grabbed a cup and poured herself a cup of the freshly brewed coffee Aaron had made. "I know it's dangerous. I need this."

"Why?"

She looked up from her coffee. Her green eyes held sadness for a quick second before she blinked it away. "I don't need to explain to you why."

"Fine. I need your passport." When it looked like she was going to argue, I explained. "The paparazzi have been waiting outside the courthouse all morning." My phone still had the morning gossip column displayed in the browser. I held it up for her to see. "Let me take your passport in, and you can get ready. We're going to be on a sailboat for three to four days."

She rolled her pretty eyes. "I know. It's not like I haven't been on one of Aaron's boats before."

"Yes, you've been on his yacht. But you know that little sailboat that hangs off the side? That is what we're taking. One of the large yachts needs multiple people to run. We can't risk hiring people we don't know. Your image is plastered on every screen. If you flee and someone finds out, there will be a reward to turn you in."

Annabella grabbed a muffin off the counter. "If you're so against me going, why are you doing this?"

I was doing it because I couldn't imagine anything happening to her, but I wasn't going to say that out loud. "Because it's my job."

Annabella's sparkling eyes dimmed. "Fine. Let me go grab my passport." She turned on her heel and left.

No matter how badly I wanted to explain the real reason, which was that she had wormed herself into my heart over the past two days, it was important that I keep her at a safe distance so I could do my job.

"Dude," Aaron muttered. "Your job?"

"I didn't lie. It's my job to get her to Nicaragua and find Nate."

He stirred the scrambled eggs in the frying pan. "It might be your job, but don't think I don't see the way you look at her."

"Does that matter?"

"Yes. You deserve to be happy."

I took the last sip of the remaining dark coffee Aaron had poured in my cup. "She's engaged."

"To a friend. She also said if we find Nate, the wedding is off."

Daisy walked in at the tail end of Aaron's statement and came over to give him a hug before she sat down on the stool next to me. "Are we talking about Annabella calling off the wedding? I think she would be perfect for you, John."

I gave Daisy the side-eye. "Like I told Annabella, this is a mission."

Annabella stormed in and threw her passport at me. Then she turned on her heel and stormed back out of the kitchen. Maybe she would be too angry to go on the trip with me.

I grabbed the keys off the counter. Daisy and Aaron meant well, but I didn't want to sit and listen to any more of their lecture. When we left Daisy's house the day before, we'd taken her car to Aaron's. It was parked behind everyone else's, so I climbed into the sleek two-door Maserati.

The passenger door swung open, and Neal slid in next to me. "Hey."

I clenched the steering wheel. "I think I can handle taking the passport in by myself."

Neal ignored me and folded his tall body into the passenger seat so he could shut the door. "I know you can, but the sheriff agreed to meet with me."

The front gates to Aaron and Neal's property opened when I neared them. Neal tapped away on his phone as I drove from Calabasas to the Los Angeles County Sheriff's Department. The judge had agreed to let me drop Annabella's passport off with the police.

The night before, Brock had called a few friends, and we were working on getting Annabella a better lawyer. She had always used Nate as her lawyer, but with everything that had gone down, we all agreed she needed to fire the lawyer her manager had recommended. Annabella ended up wanting to use Marta, Nate's sister. I still didn't think that was the best idea since we still didn't know if his family was behind Nate's disappearance. Annabella swore Marta wouldn't do anything to hurt her.

My fingers squeezed the steering wheel. When we arrived at the sheriff's office, most of the paparazzi were still standing on the steps, probably waiting for more information about Nate and Annabella. She was the talk of every gossip column. Even the local news had started to follow the case of the high-profile actress turned killer.

I parked the car close to the entrance and stared at the mass of photographers. "Don't you think it's strange that everyone is jumping to the conclusion she killed him?"

Neal glanced up from his phone. "Yes. I've been trying to track down the sources for their stories. They keep saying they have someone on the inside, which we know is not true. It seems all the info is coming from the same person. Someone is setting it up to look like she's a scorned lover."

"Nate?"

Neal shook his head. "The person isn't that good at covering their tracks. It's someone in Los Angeles. Brock said Jacob and Gabriel are all set to leave tonight, so he sent them to check out a lead I had. The sending IP address was a coffee shop in downtown Los Angeles. I'm waiting to hear back from them."

I stepped out of the expensive car and walked toward the station. The paparazzi started yelling at Neal the second he stepped out, and the mass of people began to flash pictures and yell question after question. I worked my way through the crowd. When we reached the sheriff's station, I threw open the door and let Neal in first.

"God, I hate them," he grumbled. "I'm glad they don't bother Aaron, Daisy, and me that much anymore. We used to be on their radar every time we went out for lunch. They were always asking questions about our life and how three people were in a relationship together."

"I can't wait for this case to be over."

Neal huffed. "I think you'll be sad when you have to leave Annabella."

I ignored the comment and went to the reception desk. The deputy at the desk looked as though she were in her late twenties. Her eyes grew when Neal walked up next to me. She played with her hair. "Are you Neal Ross? I can't believe you're here in person. Can I get your autograph?" When she spoke, her high-pitched voice sounded like that of a schoolgirl.

Neal rolled his eyes and ignored her question. "We're here to see Sheriff Clark," I said.

"Okay." She pouted and picked up the desk phone to let the sheriff know we were there. When she hung up, she clicked a button on the wall next to her phone. I heard a loud click come from the door to our right. The door was solid steel and creaked when I swung it open. The young girl was on the other side when we stepped through. She waved for us to follow her as she walked toward an open area lined with deputies.

Detectives and officers stared as we walked back toward the sheriff's office. I was used to being stared at. People always wanted to know how I'd gotten the scar. Then they would get mad when I said I didn't want to talk about it. But today, people were staring because Neal was walking through. I heard someone murmur about the software he'd created to help with facial recognition.

Sheriff Clark's office door was open, so Neal and I walked in. The older sheriff was sitting behind his desk. I handed him Annabella's passport before sitting down in the leather chair opposite him.

Neal took the seat next to me. "Sheriff, what have you found?"

Sheriff Clark leaned back in his chair. "No, 'hi, how are you?'"

"I figured you have things to do, as I do," Neal said. "It seems this department is concentrating more on just proving Annabella is the killer instead of finding the body."

The sheriff shifted in his seat. "Evidence points to Annabella."

Neal tapped a couple of times on his tablet then turned it so the sheriff could see. "To me, it sounds more like you're trying to do whatever Nate's dad says. So my question is, what does he have on you?"

An email between Nate's dad and the sheriff was displayed on the tablet. The email wasn't sent to the sheriff's office work email—it was his Gmail account. Neal clicked next and went to another email. "Do you want to see more, or do you get the picture?" Neal asked the sheriff.

"How did you get those? I could have you arrested."

"Fine. Have me arrested, and these will be put into evidence along with the other emails in that account. You're up for election this year. I don't think the voters will like how their sheriff is taking bribes."

Sheriff Clark's face took on a deep shade of red. His jaw twitched. "I can't stop the investigation. What do you want?"

"We never said to stop the investigation. Annabella didn't do anything. Do your job and find the person behind this." Neal stood and walked toward the door.

I couldn't believe the Los Angeles County Sheriff was doing what Nate's father wanted. I leaned across his desk. "If I find out you aren't trying to find Nate and continue down the path of Annabella, those emails will be the least of your worries."

Neal was exiting the building when I caught up. The flashes from the paparazzi were worse the second time. More media must've gotten wind we'd come down to the station. Annabella had been seen with Daisy and her men many times. The reporters yelled question after question, asking if Annabella really killed her fiancé. They followed us to the car, blocking us in.

"God, I hate the paparazzi," I growled.

"Slowly back up," Neal said. "They'll move."

I shifted the car into reverse and slowly backed up. It took a few moments, but the reporters eventually moved away from the vehicle. As soon as it was clear, we sped down the road and headed back to Daisy's house.

I shot a glance at Neal. "You didn't think to tell me he was working with Nate's dad?"

Neal looked up from his tablet. "I found it on our way in. I've been digging for it for the last twelve hours. It seemed strange that the sheriff came out saying Annabella was still under suspicion. Normally, they wouldn't give a lead up like that. The media wasn't even asking for a press conference, but he scheduled one and came out with the data."

I turned down the last road toward Daisy's. We were only a mile away from Daisy's house. We'd just come to the top of a hill when a deer darted out from the side of the road. I slammed on the brakes, but nothing happened. I swerved to miss the deer and continued to press down on the pedal, but nothing happened.

"Slow down," Neal barked next to me.

"Trying." I reached for the emergency brake and pulled. The car just continued to gain speed as we drove down the hill.

"Someone cut the brakes," I ground out.

With each second, we raced down the hill toward a sharp corner. I gripped the steering wheel, hoping we wouldn't flip as we went around the corner.

Neal gripped the dashboard as the car screeched around the corner. I felt the side of the car lift as we went. Our speed was up to seventy-five miles an hour. In about a half mile, there was another hill. I hoped we could make it there because we would lose speed as the car tried to climb.

Just then, the gas started to accelerate even without my foot on the pedal. "Neal, please tell me you hacked the car. And if not, can you?"

Neal shook his head and reached for his tablet. "It's

not me, and it will take me a few minutes to hack into the car if they didn't put up any block."

We were coming close to another car in front of us. I swerved into the other lane to pass when a semi came around the corner. There wasn't enough room to go back into my lane. I pointed the car toward the ditch.

But it wasn't a ditch. Daisy's car flew over the embankment and dropped ten feet before the wheels hit the ground. The vehicle bounced as it drove through the dense grass. I tried to turn, but the steering wheel was locked. The car hit a tree head-on. My head hit the side window, and everything went black.

9

ANNABELLA

"Red or black?" Daisy asked as she held up two different boxes of hair dye.

I reached past her and grabbed the blue dye off the shelf. John would be mad when he got back to the house and found out Daisy and I had snuck out to the store. We were being careful, though. I had my hair up under a hat, and I was wearing a massive pair of sunglasses.

The convenience store was only a few miles from the house. Even though I had just been kept inside for a day, I wanted out. And I wanted to change my hair because everyone had my picture plastered across the internet.

Daisy and I figured it would be a good idea for me to dye my hair and cut it. Since she was good at hair and makeup, I planned to let her do whatever she wanted. The producer of my latest movie might be mad when I went back to work, but I didn't know if or when that would ever happen. I made sure each of my movie contracts didn't dictate my hair color or style. That was one of my nonnegotiables. If I wanted to change my hair, a wig or extensions could be worn on a movie set to make my hair look the same.

"I love the blue, but it might stand out too much," Daisy said. "You're going to another country to find the person you're being framed for murdering."

I placed the bright-blue hair dye back on the shelf and grabbed the brown color. If we found Nate and I was cleared for his murder, I would need to dye my hair back to blond. Red would be hard to get out.

The two of us made it in and out of the store without being seen. "See? We don't need the men to do everything," I said.

"Daisy's—I mean *my* ass is going to be so red tonight. Aaron told me before he jumped in the shower that we were to wait for him."

When Daisy had been held captive for so many years, she'd started to speak about herself in the third person. When she started to date Neal and Aaron, Daisy worked with her therapist to help her stop speaking in third person. She had worked hard to stop in the past three months, but every so often, she had to catch herself. I knew she belonged to the local BDSM club. I still couldn't believe she enjoyed being a submissive after what her captor had done to her.

"Daisy, I didn't mean to get you into trouble. I'll talk with Aaron and Neal when we get home."

Daisy smiled from ear to ear. "Oh, I'm looking forward to my punishment. It's been a while since I did something this bad. Maybe Aaron will bring out the deer hide flogger."

I pulled the passenger door open and slid into the SUV. When my ass hit the seat, I heard a click followed by a ticking noise. Daisy pulled the driver's door open, but before she could climb behind the wheel, I yelled, "No! Stay out, Daisy. I need you to call John."

She backed away from the car and pulled out her phone. The ticking of what I assumed was a bomb seemed to echo through the SUV. Each tick counted down the seconds until I died. Maybe Nate really was dead. Why else would someone try to kill me? I slowly turned and watched Daisy pace back and forth.

After a few seconds, she pulled her phone away and dialed another number. Finally, she started to talk to someone. Her hand went to her mouth, and tears began to stream down her face. She nodded her head and continued to chat. Her hands were flying through the air with each word she spoke as she started toward my side of the SUV and opened the door. Finally, she took the phone away from her ear and tapped the speaker icon. "Okay, what am I looking for?"

"Do you have a mirror in your purse?" Aaron asked.

Daisy stepped back and dug through her purse until she pulled out her foundation. Then she started to lean into the car.

I shook my head vehemently. "Stop, Daisy! I don't want you to get hurt."

She ignored me and used the mirror to look under my seat. "Okay, the bomb has a clock. We have forty-five minutes. There are a lot of wires."

"Okay," Aaron answered. "Step back. I'm on my way. The second we hang up, I will call Gabriel and have him meet me there. He is one of Brock's top bomb experts. Then I will call Neal for an update. I love you, Daisy. Step back and be safe. If anything changes, call me." The phone went dead.

"What is John doing?" I asked.

Daisy looked past me, and her eyes started to water. "He will try to make it."

"Try to make it? I'm sitting on a fucking bomb. Tell me what's going on."

She still had tears running down her face. "Someone took control of the brakes and gas pedal of my car."

"I need more than that. Are they okay?"

Daisy took a deep breath. "Neal didn't tell me much. I called Neal first since he was supposed to be with John. Neal is going to stay with John. When I called Aaron, he was on his way to the accident."

Two years ago, I had a role in an action-adventure movie. There was a scene at the end in which I was tied to a chair with a bomb underneath. The ticking had seemed so real when I did the scene that it was easy to put myself into a place of danger, but the real thing was ten times scarier.

My nose itched, but I was scared to make a move. I wanted John. Over the past couple of days, he had been there to answer questions and make me feel safe. He was an overprotective ass, but at that moment, I wanted his overprotective ass to come save me from being blown up. I had no clue who Gabriel was. The only thing I knew about him was that he was going to be one of the captains on our boat along with Jacob.

"Are we sure this Gabriel is any good?"

Daisy looked up from her phone. "Brock only hires the best. Gabriel was a Navy SEAL. His specialty is in bombs."

With each tick of the bomb, my nerves frayed even more. "Daisy, you should go stand by the store. What happens if this thing goes off early or if I move and cause it to go off?"

"Not happening. When I looked, we had forty-five minutes. Now we're down to forty-two. Gabriel will be here soon and look at the bomb. Then we'll be on our way home."

"Do you think you'll get the flogger you wanted?" I needed her to keep talking to me and drown out the sound of the bomb. "I know you said earlier John went to the same club as you guys. Does that mean he's a Dom like Aaron?"

Daisy wiped the tears from her face. "Yes. John is a Dom and has been in the lifestyle since I've known him."

I was hoping for more information about the tall giant who seemed to growl at me more than smile. He didn't like that I kept wanting to put myself in danger, and for the first time, I wished I had listened to him.

"How mad do you think he's going to be at me for leaving?"

Daisy twisted her hair. "Oh, he's going to be mad. John is overprotective. He talked to Brock for an hour last night about how dangerous it is to let you come along on the mission. But I think Brock is trying to play matchmaker. We all love John to death and see the way you look at each other."

I didn't need a mirror to know my face was bright red. "You think he likes me?"

"Yes. But you are going to make the first move." Daisy scanned the parking lot. "How do you think they put the bomb in so fast?"

"I don't know. It's almost like it had to be done before we left the house. How did the bomb just now engage?"

I knew little about technology, but I knew no one had snuck into the driveway. Neal, one of Daisy's fiancés, kept the front yard and house locked down better than most government security facilities. Hell, the government used his technology to help protect Langley. The only other option was that someone had followed us when we left the house and had planted the bomb when we went in the store.

I looked around as much as I could without moving. "Do you see any cameras?" Maybe we could catch a break and find out who was trying to kill me.

Daisy stepped back from the car. I wanted to turn and watch, but I was too scared to move a muscle. My body ached from sitting ramrod straight in the same position. I could feel a trickle of sweat dripping down my face. More droplets fell with each second that passed. Five minutes felt like six hours.

"I didn't see any—" Daisy's words were cut off by the squeal of tires. "Gabriel is here."

My body loosened a little now that someone was there who could help me. But my mind went back to John. I wanted to know if he was hurt, and if so, how bad.

I heard a car door slam followed by the sound of heavy footsteps. With each tick of the clock, I heard another step. Time crept by as I waited for the man named Gabriel to come diffuse the bomb.

A tall man stood next to me. He had to duck down to see into the car. His hair was cut in a short military style, not long like John's. His eyes were dark brown, almost black. "Hi, Annabella. I'm Gabriel. I was hoping to meet you on better terms tonight, but let's take a look at this bomb."

"Oh, you mean better terms as in trying to help me flee the country to find the man I'm being accused of killing?"

The younger man let out a bark of laughter. "True. Let's see what we're working with." Gabriel leaned into the SUV and looked between my legs at the bomb under my seat. Any other time, I might be excited to have a young man between my legs. But at that moment, I wanted John by my side and the bomb under my seat gone.

Gabriel stood up and ran his hand through his hair. "Okay, Annabella, I'm going to grab the tools I need from the truck and come back in a second."

I reached out and grabbed his shirt. "Wait. Is John coming?"

He looked back toward his truck. "Let's get this bomb taken care of." Gabriel was jogging to his SUV before I could ask another question.

With each second that ticked by, I wondered if I would ever be able to see John again. If I made it out of this mess, I wanted to plant a big kiss on John. Even if we found Nate, I didn't plan on marrying him. Hell, I didn't know if I even wanted to be friends with him again. I closed my eyes and leaned back against the headrest, not understanding how we ended up this way. A few days ago, I was planning a wedding to my best friend and starring in my next blockbuster hit. Now I was wanted for murder and sitting on a bomb.

The bomb expert, Gabriel, returned with a bag. In the movie I had starred in that had the bomb under my seat, the person who'd pretended to be disarming it had worn a full-body bomb suit. Gabriel was dressed in a black T-shirt and dark jeans.

"Shouldn't you be in a bomb suit?" I asked as I wiped my sweaty hands down my jeans.

"If we were back in Ft. Lauderdale, where I have my stuff, then yes. But I don't travel with a bomb suit. Okay, let me get this diffused. We're down to thirty minutes, and this might take me a while."

"Then why don't we call the police? They should have bomb people. I don't want you to get hurt."

Gabriel leaned his hip against the open door. "With what happened to John and Neal, we aren't sure we can trust the police."

"Someone needs to tell me what the hell is going on. Are John and Neal okay?"

"John will be okay. Now let me do my job so he doesn't kick my ass for not getting this bomb diffused." Gabriel lay down on the passenger side floor. His arm brushed against my leg, causing me to jump.

I held my breath for a few seconds, waiting for the bomb to go off. When nothing happened, I exhaled. "How's it going down there?" I asked while I watched

Daisy pace outside the car with her phone attached to her ear.

"I've seen this type of bomb before. I should have it diffused in a couple more minutes."

With no one telling me how John was, I slowly reached out and grabbed my phone from my purse. The screen flashed with a low battery signal when I unlocked it. The battery was at one percent when I clicked on the phone icon, and my phone died. I leaned back and closed my eyes, when I heard another car pulling up. Daisy ran to the newcomer. I couldn't see who it was unless I twisted in my seat.

Aaron stood next to the door.

"Where's John?" I asked.

He ran his hand through his hair and ignored my question. "How are you doing, Gabriel?"

I wanted to launch myself at him in frustration. "Hello? I asked a question."

"Good until a second ago when I cut the wrong wire," Gabriel said. "Time's going down a little faster. Might want to back up and get Daisy out of here."

"How much time?" I asked. When he didn't answer, I was tempted to kick him. "Time, Gabriel."

Gabriel rolled out from under my seat and grabbed my hand. "We need to run now." He yanked me out of the car, and I tried to keep up with him. He was running so fast, he was practically dragging me. Aaron and Daisy sprinted in front of us. We were twenty feet from the car when it exploded, and we flew forward. Gabriel grabbed me and tucked me under him as we hit the pavement and rolled. His back hit the asphalt with a thud. My knee skidded across the cement. Smoke billowed, and debris rained down around us.

I rolled off of Gabriel and onto my back. "I thought you could diffuse the bomb."

He ran a hand over his face. "They put in a trip wire I didn't see. When I cut the cord for the seat, the clock cut the time to one minute. It was easier to pull you out than to worry about saving the car.

Aaron and Daisy walked over and helped us stand up. Sirens blared down the street. The police would be there soon.

"Are you guys okay?" Aaron asked.

"Yes," Gabriel and I both responded.

Aaron held Daisy close to him. "Daisy, I need you to take them to the hospital and get them both checked out. I'll stay and wait for the police then take an Uber to the hospital. I don't want them to know Annabella is here. Something is going on, and until we know what, I want to keep any information close to the vest."

10

JOHN

My head pounded like a set of drums. I heard voices, but I couldn't make anything out. Taking a couple of deep breaths, I opened my eyes. Annabella was sitting next to my bed. *Fuck, I'm in the hospital.* That was the last place I wanted to be. I tried to sit up when another hand pushed me back down.

"John, you need to stay in bed," Aaron said. "Let me get the doctor to come check you out."

"How long have I been out?" The accident came back in one quick flash. The brakes hadn't worked, and the car had hit the tree head-on. I reached up and touched the side of my head, feeling a large bump where I'd hit the window.

Neal leaned against the wall. "A couple hours. You scared the shit out of me when you wouldn't wake up. After the crash, I called 911 and then Aaron."

Annabella reached over and grabbed my hand. Her hand felt so warm, but my body went cold when I saw the bandage on her forehand and the scrape along her arm. "What happened?"

She bit her lip. The gesture stirred a desire I didn't have time to deal with. "It was nothing."

Neal and Jacob coughed on the other side of the room. Daisy turned her head so I couldn't see her face.

"Tell me what happened." When she tried to pull away, I gripped her hand.

She fidgeted for a moment before she answered. "Someone planted a bomb in Daisy's SUV."

I laid my head back and closed my eyes. The throbbing in my head got worse with each second. *A bomb.* And I wasn't there to make sure she was okay. "I take it you weren't able to disarm the bomb," I said to Gabriel. I couldn't hold back the coldness in my voice. He was one of the best bomb experts in the Navy. He still went and helped teach the new cadets, and the local Ft. Lauderdale police used his expertise.

Gabriel ran his hand across his short-cropped hair. "When I disarmed the pressure switch to the seat, the time cut to one minute. Instead of trying to disarm it, I pulled her out of the car to make sure I could get her away. My main goal was to get Annabella out of danger, man. I'd seen the bomb configuration before. It shouldn't have done what it did. I've been racking my brain, trying to figure out what went wrong, and the only thing I could think of was that they messed up building it. I'm glad I got her out of there when I did. Who knows if it would've counted down correctly?"

"Fuck! So someone messed with the car and put a bomb in the SUV. Was this done at Neal's house?"

Neal planted himself in the chair by the window. One of his arms was in a sling, and the other hand flew across the keyboard. It looked like he was working just as fast as he did with two arms. "No. I checked the video. Somehow, the video feed from the sheriff's office is gone. There was a glitch during the time we were talking to the sheriff. The video near the convenience store had the same issue."

Annabella gasped next to me. When I looked over, she appeared worried. I wanted to pull her into my arms and promise her everything would be okay.

"Who could be doing this?" she asked.

I squeezed her hand before turning back to Gabriel. "Whose signature was on the bomb?"

"I've seen it used in another mob case."

My jaw hardened. "So those men leaving Nate's office are behind this?"

Gabriel paced in front of the hospital bed. "That was my first thought, but whoever built the bomb wasn't an expert, and when the mob tries to off some-one, they do it correctly. Because if the person they hire messes up, that person is taken out. This bomb wasn't built correctly."

"Do you really think the mob is trying to kill me?" Annabella's lip started to tremble. "Maybe Nate is dead and the info we found is wrong."

I couldn't hold back any longer. I tugged her from the chair onto my bed. Neal looked up from the laptop and smirked. She didn't protest and snuggled up next to me.

"We still need to go to Nicaragua and look into the info Neal found," I said. "And I'm not letting you out of my sight until we figure out what is going on. So it looks like I'm not going to complain any longer about you coming with."

Neal tapped his fingers on the keys. "Jacob went to the private airfield to get set up. We have a four-seat cargo plane waiting to take you to Nicaragua in the morning. I picked up Annabella's fake passport. She will need to dye her hair tonight. We don't want any chance of her being recognized. We don't have time for you guys to sail there on a boat. The fastest way is to try to sneak you out of the country by plane."

Waiting until morning wouldn't be helpful. We needed to handle the situation tonight. "Why can't we leave now?"

Gabriel shook his head. "Dude, you have a concussion. You can't leave until morning."

I narrowed my eyes at him. "I can handle my

concussion. And when did you go from calling me sir to dude?"

Gabriel shrugged. "It's been a long day. I'm going to grab something to eat then go help Jacob. If you need anything, let us know."

Annabella tapped me on the shoulder. "You should be nicer to him. He saved my life today."

The thought of Annabella almost dying had my nerves on edge. It would be hard to control myself if we find Nate. In fact, it would take everything in me not to kill the fucker. How could someone leave Annabella with all of this baggage?

Aaron and the doctor walked in a couple of minutes after Gabriel left. They didn't say anything about the fact that Annabella was next to me. I wasn't about to give them a chance. She settled something inside me. Having her next to me felt perfect. We would need to discuss what was happening between us. After hearing she could have died, I had an overwhelming need to protect her. Annabella deserved to be with someone who cared about her and didn't leave her with the possibility of being set up for murder.

"Good evening, Mr. Waters," the doctor said.

Annabella tried to scoot out of bed, but I tightened my grip around her waist.

"When can I get out of here?"

The doctor smiled. "I can always tell when I have

an ex-military man as a patient. They never even ask what's wrong, just 'when can I leave?' "

"I feel fine," I grumbled.

The doctor opened the chart and glanced at it. "You have a concussion and were unconscious for a couple hours. I want to watch over you for a couple more hours. Then you can go home as long as you have someone to watch you tonight."

"What do I need to do?" Annabella asked.

The doctor handed her a piece of paper with information on concussions and what to look out for. "If you need anything else, please don't hesitate to ask." He nodded to me. "Thank you for your service." Then he turned and left.

"If I'm going to be released in a couple hours, I think we should leave tonight."

Aaron leaned forward in his chair. "No. I already talked to Brock. They're working on gathering more information before you head down. You will be fine going in the morning. You took a good hit to the head —you don't need to be jetting off tonight. We want to make sure you have to even go. Brock has a contact down there who's going to see if they can get a glimpse of Nate before you leave."

Annabella laid her head down on my shoulder and grabbed my hand. "I agree with Brock, let's go tomorrow. Don't get me wrong—I want to figure out what is going on—but your health is more important."

Neal cursed from the chair. "You might want to call your sister."

Confusion furrowed my brow. "Why?"

Neal reached for the controller and turned on the TV. My face flashed across the screen. The news anchors were discussing whether Annabella and I were having an affair and if that might be the reason she'd killed him or had him murdered.

"The news media is talking about you and Annabella dating. She's probably already arranged the wedding. We all know how much Addie loves Annabella," Neal said as a picture of me and Annabella on the sheriff's office steps flashed across the screen. "You know the media will be hounding her for answers."

"I'll call her in a few. I don't understand why they are so adamant he's dead." I grumbled.

Missing money, and no body all led me to think he was still alive. With someone trying to kill us, I believed he was running from something. I just didn't know why they would go after Annabella. We needed to figure out what he was running from.

"Deep down, I have this feeling he's still alive," Annabella said. "But when we do find him, I might kill him for leaving me with this mess. I wish he would have told me what was wrong or what was going on."

I didn't plan on letting Annabella dirty her hands by killing her ex-fiancé. I would do it myself. I planned

to find Nate and let Annabella call off the fake engagement before I persuaded her to be mine. Hopefully,
she could overlook the scar down the side of my face.

Daisy looked down at her phone. "John, are you
going to call your sister?"

"I don't know where my phone is. I need it to call
her."

"You can use mine." Annabella started to get up to
get her phone, but I pulled her back to my side.

"Neal, can you grab Annabella's phone?"

Neal set his laptop to the side and tossed me the
phone. "Don't get used to this. I did that because you're
still supposed to be in bed."

I looked over at Annabella. "Are you sure you want
me to use your phone to call my sister? She might call
you once she has your number."

She rolled her pretty green eyes. "Call her."

Addie picked up on the first ring. "Hello?" Her
voice sounded worried.

"Hey, pip-squeak."

Addie let out a deep breath. "You know how many
times I've tried to call you? I was about to book a flight.
Do you know what that means for me to even go to the
airline's website and start looking for one? Nobody
would tell me anything. All I keep seeing on the gossip
rags is a picture of you being carted off, John. What the
hell is going on?"

My throat closed up. "You almost booked a flight?"

The line was quiet for a second. "Yes." That was all I needed to hear to know how worried she was. A flight for Addie would have been really hard for her.

"I'm fine. A couple stitches and a concussion. Annabella is going to watch me tonight. But I might not be able to talk for a few days. We need to figure out who's after her."

I heard the rustling of papers on the other end of the phone. If I were a betting man, I would bet she contacted Brock, got information on Annabella's case, and spent the last few hours looking to see what she could find. When her anxiety increased, research helped keep her mind off the surrounding problems.

"He didn't leave the country," Addie said.

"Who?" I had a feeling I knew who she was going to say, but I wanted to hear the words from her. Neal motioned for me to put the phone on speaker, so I tapped the screen.

"Nate," Addie answered.

Neal set his laptop to the side. "What have you found, pip-squeak?"

I could almost see Addie roll her eyes. "I'm not a pip-squeak. You guys need to stop calling me that. I understand why you think he might've gone to Nicaragua, but I pulled security footage from the night he and Pedro left. They didn't head towards an airport or the boat docks. When they left, they went north on the 495 towards Santa Clarita. Last year, Nate bought a house in Santa Clarita and signed it over to Pedro."

Annabella gasped. I pulled her in closer, and she laid her head on my chest.

"Were you able to find any camera footage showing they're in Santa Clarita?" I asked.

"No."

Now we had two possible locations they could be, and we needed to decide which one to visit. "Thanks for the info, pip-squeak." Addie huffed on the other end, making me smirk. "Let us know if you find anything else. Be careful."

"You too, big bro." The line went dead.

Neal had picked his laptop back up, and I used Annabella's phone to call Brock.

"Addie gave us another lead."

The sound of the keyboard clicking in the background let me know Brock was in his usual location— in front of his monitors, looking at the world. "Yeah, we talked earlier. I planned to call you when the doctor let you go. I'm doing some more research. Call me when you get back to Daisy's house."

"Okay."

The next couple of hours moved slow. I wanted to get out of the hospital room and figure out a plan. Neal and I had come up with an idea—I would go to Santa Clarita and see what I could find, while Gabriel and

Jacob would head to Nicaragua to see if they could come up with another lead.

Annabella had fallen asleep on my chest. I liked having her in my arms. The doctor finally walked back in to let us know a nurse would be by with the discharge papers. Annabella woke up and climbed off the bed. It felt so empty without her next to me.

I was changing back into my regular clothes when Annabella's phone rang. Her face went from pale to bright red as she looked at the display. She angrily swiped her finger across the screen. "Where the fuck are you?" she screamed into the phone.

I mouthed for her to put it on speaker.

"They're going to kill me."

11

ANNABELLA

I was no longer shocked that Nate had called. Anger had replaced all the feelings I had for the man. I might've screamed at him for a good ten minutes before I let him talk. Telling him our pretend engagement was off hadn't needed to be said at that point, but I'd done it anyway. I had let out a week's worth of anger, sadness, and betrayal into one conversation.

The part that hurt the most was that Nate hadn't called because he'd wanted to clear my name. He'd figured he would help clear my name when he was no longer running from the men after him. No, he'd called because he wanted to know if Brock could help him. His location had been found, and he and Pedro were on the run again. My jaw hurt from clenching it. John had agreed to help Nate the second he'd asked.

John looked up from the map on the dining room table. We had only been home from the hospital for an hour, and John was back to work, trying to help my ex-best friend find safety. I wanted Nate to go to the police, but he was convinced they were one of the reasons he was running. And what made me mad was that he wouldn't tell us who he was running from or why people were after him.

"Why are you mad, Annabella?" John asked. "I thought you would want to help your friend."

"He's the reason you got hurt. A bomb was put in my car. And now you're helping him run when the media and police think I killed him. Why aren't we demanding that he turn himself in? The man I spoke to on the phone earlier is not the friend I used to know. He's a selfish ass." I reached up and wiped the tears from my eyes.

John walked over and pulled me into his arms. My hands pressed against his hard chest. He ran his hand down the side of my face, and the gentle touch made me fall for him even more. "I'm not helping him for his own good. We're getting him to a safe location so he'll tell us what's going on. Tomorrow, we will go and see him. I will make him give proof of life, or I will haul him in. But Annabella, whoever is after him is also after you. I'm not doing this to clear his name. Really, I don't care what happens to him, but we need to figure out who is behind this so you're no longer in danger."

When he put it like that, it made sense. "Oh."

He leaned in closer, and I ran my tongue across my lips. "Oh? Is that all you have to say?" The corner of his mouth turned up. He rested one hand on my hip, and I couldn't hold back any longer. I leaned forward and pressed my lips to his. John ran his hand through my hair, bringing me in closer as he deepened the kiss. My body felt like it was going to melt.

John pulled back and rested his forehead against mine. "What are you doing to me, Annabella?"

Before I could answer, Neal came through the kitchen door. I tried to pull back, but John kept a tight grip around my waist. Neal set his computer on the table. "John, do you have a sec?"

John grabbed my hand and pulled me over to the table. When I went to sit in the chair next to him, he pulled me onto his lap. Things felt right with John. When I was around him, I felt safe and protected, unlike the men I'd tried to date in Hollywood over the years. Jake Gilinger was the last man I'd dated before I decided to marry Nate. The more I thought back to the time I had agreed to marry Nate, I realized it might've been to get back at Jake more than to help out my friend.

Jake and I had dated for six months. We'd met on a dating app when he'd been working as a bank manager. I didn't know he was trying to become an actor until it was too late. I took him to my movie premiere and introduced him to some producers and other friends in the business. Four months into our relationship, he told me he got a movie deal. I didn't think much about it. I was happy for him. But once the ink dried on the contract, he stopped calling. Then I'd seen his picture in the tabloids saying he and his long-time girlfriend were getting married.

My gut clenched at the thought of being used. *Will John do that?*

When he looked at me, it was with concern. "Do you not like the plan?"

"What plan?" I hadn't heard a word he or Neal had said.

"We're leaving first thing in the morning and meeting Nate and Pedro at the base of Kagel Canyon." He ran his hand down my arm. "If you don't want to see Nate, you don't have to go."

"I want to go. I have so much more to say."

John tilted his head. "Are you sure? I need to know if something is bothering you."

I placed a fake smile on my face. "Everything is fine."

He looked like he wanted to say more but turned back to Neal. They were looking at a map of the area where we planned to meet Nate. I glanced up at the clock and saw that it was close to midnight. I couldn't hold back a yawn.

"Let's get you to bed." John's demanding tone did

something to my body. I wasn't used to demands, but when he did it, I wanted to melt at his feet.

John and Neal finished up their plans, and we walked upstairs. The doctor had said John would need to be woken up every few hours. Our rooms were across from each other at Daisy's house. John leaned down and gave me a kiss on the lips before he turned and walked through his door. I hurried into my room. I threw the lid to my suitcase open and searched for something cute to wear to bed. John wouldn't know what hit him.

A soft knock sounded on the door. "Come in." I didn't need to look up from the suitcase to know it was Daisy.

She padded across the room and sat cross-legged on the bed while I continued to throw the clothes from my suitcase onto the bed. "Whatcha looking for?"

I glanced up from the suitcase. "Something to wear for bed."

"It takes this much work to find something to change into? You already threw like five possible pj's to the side."

My suitcase was now empty with no options. I sat on the bed next to Daisy. "I need to stay in John's room tonight and check on him."

She grinned. "You know you could set the alarm and walk in every couple hours. You don't need to stay in the same room."

What she said was correct, but I was afraid he might need something in the night and I wouldn't be there to help him when he did. "I'm going to sleep in the chair in his room."

"Really? The chair?" Daisy held up her hand. "You like him, don't you?"

"Yes. But what happens if he uses me?"

"For what?"

I grabbed a white tank top and a pair of boy shorts from the pile of clothes. "It seems every man I date uses me to get into the industry."

Daisy burst out laughing. "You really think John would use you to become a Hollywood star? He thinks no one wants to truly be with him because of the scar. He thinks women take pity on him. Half of the women at the club would do anything to be his sub."

Jealous rage came over me for a second. "The whole sub thing scares me. I don't want to give up control."

Daisy laid her hand on my leg. "Annabella, I love you to death, but I'm protective of John. He was one of the men who rescued me, and I stayed with him over a year. If you truly see yourself with him, go for it. But if this is a fling, be up front. Don't hurt him."

"I like him, but where could this really go? I live in California, and he lives in Florida. It's not like we can go on dates. When he came to the jail to pick me up,

Daisy, I just knew he was something special. What can I do?"

"If it's meant to be and you really like him, see where it goes these next few days. When you aren't filming, you can go to Florida. And when he isn't off in another country on a secret mission, he can come to visit you."

My stomach dropped as I thought about how he put himself in danger for his job. How would I handle not getting to talk to him for days and not knowing if he was okay? I knew one thing—I couldn't say unless we talked and tried. I wasn't even sure how he felt or if he thought something was between us.

I grabbed my clothes and headed for the bathroom. Then I quickly changed into my pj's, brushed my teeth, and scrubbed the makeup off my face. When I looked in the mirror, I contemplated putting it back on. I didn't like going to bed with makeup on, and I supposed it would be dark anyway. I pulled my blond hair up into a ponytail and headed back to the bedroom.

Daisy looked up from her phone and whistled. "You're going to knock him out, girl."

I could feel my face blush. "Should I change?"

"Hell no, girl."

I grabbed the blanket off the bed and headed across the hall to John's room. The door was ajar. I lightly knocked, and he said to come in. I didn't know what I expected to see, but it wasn't John sitting up in bed with no shirt on. The bedside light was on, giving a light glow to the room. I stopped short, and my tongue ran over my lips. John raised a brow.

"Um, the doctor said someone needs to watch you at night. I planned to sleep in the chair. Or I can come back every few hours. I just thought it would be easier if I slept in your room. Is that okay? I'm trying not to impose."

"You're fine. Come in. But you don't have to sleep in the chair. You can sleep in the bed if you want. I promise to keep my hands to myself."

My palms started to sweat at the idea of sleeping next to him. My feet seemed to be rooted in place. "Okay," my voice squeaked. I placed the blanket next to the bed, and when I padded over to the side of the king-sized bed, John pulled back the covers. All he wore were black boxer briefs. I climbed into the bed next to him and scooted to the edge. I worried my hand might jet out and feel his abs. He didn't just have a six-pack. No, they went down below the covers.

John had his hair pulled up into a bun. His book lay in his lap. I wanted to run my fingers down the scar on his face. I didn't understand why he thought it made him unattractive. It turned me on and made me want to crawl on top of him and lick his chest.

When my eyes traveled down his face to that broad chest, I noticed that little scars lined his body. I didn't even realize I'd reached out until I was dragging my finger along the scar on his right pec. He jumped when my finger touched his skin.

"Can I ask you something?" I whispered.

John pinched the bridge of his nose. "If I say no, are you going to ask anyway."

My lips twitched. "Yes." I kept tracing the scars on his chest. "I know you don't know me very well or what is going on with us. But can you tell me how you got these?"

John grabbed my wrist as I went to trace another scar. "It's not a good story." He let out a sigh. "I'm not the hero in the story."

"I want to hear it anyway. For some reason, I highly doubt you're the villain either."

John didn't say a word for a good two minutes. I didn't think he would tell me what happened. But finally, he started speaking. "Three years ago, I was sent on a rescue mission to Galkayo. Did you see the story about Caleb Anderson's family?"

I remembered a story about Mr. Anderson's wife and daughters being kidnapped by Somali pirates. I leaned my head against John's chest. I wanted to be close to him as he told the story. "His wife died, right?"

"Yes," John huffed. "The mission went like any other. This wasn't our first time rescuing people kidnapped by Somali pirates. We parachuted in two miles outside of Gadaado. The team and I trekked two miles through the sandy terrain until we made it to the small village. It was full of pirates. The intel we received let us know the Andersons were being housed in one of the outer houses. They had already requested ransom from Caleb."

I'd heard about the ransom request on the news. "They wanted ten million dollars."

"Yes, and Caleb had no problem paying it. The people who took his wife and daughters wouldn't release them once he paid. So we went to rescue them." John pinched the bridge of his nose. "We were a mile from our extraction point when one of our team-mates turned on us. He put a gun to the little girl's head and tried to take her away. The mom screamed and ran towards her daughter. The area we were walking through was full of land mines. We were walking in front so they wouldn't step on one. We had a device to tell us where to walk. When she ran for her daughter, the mine blew sharp metal. That is where my scars came from. Caleb's wife died, and the man who betrayed our team took off with the little girl and left the team. I told my team to go after them. I lay on the ground, bleeding out next to Caleb's wife. One of the soldiers stayed back and helped keep pressure on my wounds."

"None of that is your fault."

"Don't you see? I was the team leader. I should've

known my team." John closed his eyes. "I should've seen he was having troubles. That's on me."

"Did you get the girls back?"

"Yes. But we lost the mom because of me. Now that girl will have to grow up knowing what it's like to watch your mom die in front of your eyes."

"John, none of this is your fault." When he started to protest, I placed my lips on his, catching his next words in my mouth.

12

JOHN

Her kiss ignited the fire burning inside me. I slid my hand down her perfect body until it rested on her hip, then I rolled her to the side so she was facing me. I pulled her body closer to me and spread my hand across her tight ass. When I tugged her closer, she draped her leg over my hip.

Her hands running over my body made it hard to think straight. When she grabbed my ass, my intense need to take control and possess her came to the forefront. Our tongues tangled. I could taste her cherry ChapStick. I deepened the kiss, and she moaned against my lips.

Annabella pulled back, and her green eyes sparkled in the night. She leaned forward and nipped my lip. I slowly dragged my fingers along the bottom of her tank top and lifted it up over her perky breasts. She sat up and finished taking her shirt off.

"Beautiful." I pulled her back into my arms and pressed my lips to hers. My need to take control was overpowering. I wanted to tie her to the bed and love her body for hours. I took a couple of deep breaths and tamped down my need. We had all night, and I planned to spend it worshipping her body.

When Annabella bit her lower lip, my focus went to her luscious lips. I couldn't wait for her to wrap them around my cock. As if reading my mind, her pink tongue shot out, and she licked her lips. I lifted Annabella over me so she straddled my legs. She rubbed herself along my member.

She lowered her pink lips until I felt them against my mouth. I tangled my hands through her hair and pulled her close. I put my other hand on her waist to keep her in place. She moved her hips against me. My control was thinning with each thrust she made against me.

"Stop," I whispered against her mouth. Her hips stilled. "I don't want to come yet. You're so beautiful. It's taking everything in me to hold back."

She smiled and slowly kissed her way down my body, stopping right above my briefs and tracing her tongue along the top of my waistband. Annabella worked her fingers under the waistband of my briefs and slowly pulled them down my legs until she had them off. She slowly crawled back up the bed, kissing my thigh. She wrapped her hands around my member.

I threw my head back, letting out a groan. Her silky hands felt good. I opened my eyes to see her watching my every move. She licked her lips before she lowered her head and wrapped her soft pink lips around me. The pleasure was pure bliss. I reached down and wrapped my fingers in her hair. A slight moan escaped her lips, sending a vibration through her throat as she took me deeper in her mouth.

"Beautiful, look at me."

Annabella's green eyes snapped open. I wasn't the only one lost in the arousal and lust. She picked up the pace as she kept her eyes trained on me. I pulled her head up for a second, needing to get myself under control. I was close to needing release. Annabella must've known she had me on edge. She lowered her lips back to my cock and took me even deeper into her mouth. She worked her tongue along the edge. Everything she did was better than I had ever experienced.

"God, Beautiful, I don't know if I can last much longer. Your lips feel so good."

Instead of slowing her down, my words seemed to spark a fire inside of her. She dug her nails into my butt and pulled me closer. Her velvet mouth was too much. I was about to lose control.

I reached down and dragged her up my body. She

straddled my waist. I pulled her mouth to mine, and our tongues danced. I reached up and caressed her nipples. She moaned into my mouth.

"I need you undressed." My voice sounded strained, even to my own ears.

She still had her boy shorts on. She stood and turned so her ass was facing me then slowly bent over and dragged her shorts down her shapely legs, giving me a perfect view of her tight ass. I couldn't hold back. I brought my hand down on her creamy white flesh. She let out a yelp at first and then didn't move.

"Did you like that, Beautiful?"

"Yes," she whispered shyly.

I brought my hand down a couple more times, and her skin started to turn a lovely shade of pink. I could hear her panting.

"Turn around and come here."

I sat up before she could straddle me again and slowly licked her clit. Her legs shook as she tried to stand still. She reached for the bed post so she could continue to stand. I lightly blew on her clit, and her body shuddered with each breath. I slowly took her nub into my mouth and sucked. Annabella moaned. Her legs were quivering.

"You're so wet for me." I sucked on her pearl for a few more seconds. "Why don't you lie down on the bed?"

Annabella lay next to me. I leaned down and took

her nipple into my mouth. Her hips arched off the bed. When I ran my finger through her folds, she moaned my name. I loved the sound of my name coming off her lips.

I let go of her nipple and worked my way down her body. With each kiss, she let out a frustrated sigh. When I looked up, her pretty green eyes were shut tight.

"Open your eyes, Annabella. I want you to watch me devour your body."

I could feel goose bumps form on her skin as I ran my hands down her body. When I kneeled between her legs, I put one of her knees over each of my shoulders then leaned down and licked her folds. She tried to arch for more contact, but I moved back and swatted her thigh.

"Stop trying to take more."

"I'm so close John. Please, I need to come."

I took her nub in my mouth and nipped it. Her breathing picked up. It seemed my temptress liked a little pain with her pleasure. After the spankings, she was dripping with need and desire. My dick was so hard as I thought about sliding into her.

"I don't want you to come yet."

She propped herself up on her elbows and watched as I slid my index finger into her. Her velvety folds sucked my fingers in, wanting more. Annabella flopped back on the bed and let out a frustrated sigh. I would bring her almost to the brink of an orgasm and pull back.

"John, I can't hold on much longer."

Wanting to feel her come on my hand, I added a second finger and pumped them in and out of her. I bit down on her nub harder than before, and she screamed my name as she rode my hand. Her hips were off the bed, looking for and needing more.

"I'm coming. Fuck!" She exploded on my tongue.

Watching her fall apart was the most erotic thing I had ever seen. I wanted to see it happen again. I continued to suck on her clit. I pinched her right nipple and rubbed it between my fingers.

"I need more. I need you, John. Please..."

The desperation in her voice made me stop. I slowly kissed my way up her body, stopping at her nipple and taking it into my mouth. She wrapped her legs around my waist and rubbed her sex against me. Her breath was coming short and fast. I leaned down and kissed her neck, working my way up so I could nibble on her ear.

"Please, John."

I was so wrapped up in the passion that I almost forgot about protection. "Hang on." I had to grab a condom. I reached into the nightstand next to the bed, hoping Neal or Aaron had condoms there.

Desire clouded Annabella's features. "I need you now." I could see the need in her eyes and body.

"I need to grab a condom."

Her eyes widened as if she had completely forgotten. "Oh God, I can't believe I didn't think about that. I'm not on the pill."

I found a condom and ripped open the wrapper. Her pretty green eyes watched my every move. "Do you want to put it on?"

She bit her lip and nodded. Her hands reached out and grabbed the condom then slowly rolled it down my length. Her soft hands were almost my undoing.

Once she had me sheathed, she ran her hands up and down my length a couple more times. I couldn't hold back—I needed to be inside her.

The connection between us was strong. I sank into her and didn't stop until I was all the way in. She was so tight and felt so good. Sex with Annabella was better than anything I could have ever imagined.

Her eyes opened. "Move, John. I want to feel you move inside me."

I flexed my hips, meeting her heated flesh.

"Please," she begged with each thrust. Her breathy moan almost caused me to come. "I need you." With every thrust, a moan escaped her luscious lips. Annabella raised her knees and wrapped her ankles around my back. With the new position, I went deeper inside of her. She met each of my thrusts and tightened herself each time.

My breathing was erratic. I reached between us and pinched her clit. She screamed out my name as she went over the edge. Her voice was loud and raspy. Her muscles pulsed, and she ground against me to drag out her climax. God, it felt like a silky explosion. I couldn't wait to do this again.

"John…"

I was lost in passion, chasing my own orgasm. My hips thrust hard, and my ass flexed with each thrust. Neither of us expected her to come again. When her muscles tightened around me, I lost control and went over the edge with her.

I rested my forehead against hers, trying to catch my breath. We were both breathing heavy. When I rolled off of her and moved to get off the bed, Annabella whined at the loss of connection.

"I will be right back." I tied off the condom and threw it in the trash before I snuggled back into bed next to Annabella. She pressed her body against mine.

I slowly dragged my finger along her arm. "I have a question for you, Annabella."

"Hmm." She was still in an orgasm-induced coma.

"Did you like when I spanked you?" I hadn't planned on doing anything from the BDSM lifestyle, even on a small scale, until we'd talked about it.

She covered her face with her hands. "I didn't think I would, but I really liked it."

I tugged her hands down. "You have nothing to be embarrassed about." I pulled her over so I could capture her lips.

We spent the rest of the night making love.

13

ANNABELLA

"**A**re you ready?" John asked from the driver's side.

Over the past three days, a lot had changed. Neal and Addie had worked together to dig through Nate's computer and phone records. When they found Nate had been talking with the mafia, Addie dug deeper into the crime family. It seemed the mob kept records of gambling debts digitally. From the movies, I assumed they only kept gambling debts in a notebook, locked in a safe.

Nate's dad was in debt to the mafia. When Addie and Neal had found the information, Neal contacted Marta. She admitted her dad was in deep with the crime family. She didn't think the mafia would actually kill Nate. Marta said the crime family had sent someone to her house to scare her into telling her dad he needed to pay up and to show they could get to Marta. Her dad hadn't paid up. Nate had and he stayed with the firm to keep an eye on his sister even though she'd hired her own security. Nate's family trust was monitored by Nate, and he gave his dad an allowance that was nothing close to what the man owed. So his dad had started to use the law firm to repay the gambling debt. After Nate tried to stop taking the cases, I'd found him almost beaten to death. I wished Nate would have hired his own security. The mafia thought if they made it look like they'd killed Nate, he would come out of hiding. Nate's dad's debt had grown, and instead of paying, he had run.

Last week, he lost a case, and one of the top men in the mafia was now going to prison for life. When Nate left the courthouse, he was taken and beaten again. The blood I'd found in the bathroom was from a wound that wouldn't stop bleeding. Vito had also sent people to Pedro's house to let Nate know they could get to him. They were sending a message that he should never lose another case.

Luckily, John and Neal had met with Vito the day before to discuss what was going on. Neal showed Vito the evidence he'd found against the mob and threatened to turn it over to the police. It was a bluff on our part. The sheriff couldn't use the evidence we collected because we'd gotten it without warrants. Vito was surprised to find out about the bomb and the cut brakes. He also said they'd never contacted Pedro's mom. So someone was still trying to frame me for murder and wanted access to the video in the house.

Vito told John that he'd called Carmine to come find Nate, not kill him. The older mobster went on to explain he would rather have Nate alive and working for him. After a lengthy discussion, the mobster agreed they would not make Nate take any more criminal cases. Neal was going to hold on to a copy of the evidence we had against the mob just in case we needed it in the future.

The car bomb and Nate running had nothing to do with the other. The mob swore up and down they weren't the ones who'd contacted the police or Pedro's mom. But someone was still working on framing me.

Nate had agreed to meet us at the sheriff's office to prove he was alive and clear my name.

"Let's do this, and then we can get back to our lives." I tried to keep a smile on my face as I said the last part. John and I had had lots of mind-blowing sex over the past three days, but we hadn't talked about what might happen when my case was completely cleared. I reached for the handle of the rented SUV.

John met me halfway around the SUV and grabbed my hand. "It will be okay, Beautiful."

He pulled the doors to the station open for me. I hadn't been back since the day I was arrested and the deputy took me to a small room to ask me questions about murdering my fiancé. The lady behind the counter sneered when she saw me, but the second her eyes landed on John, she sat up straighter and ran her fingers through her hair. I wanted to claw her eyes out. I still didn't understand how the man didn't see how hot he was.

John walked up to the desk. "We're here to see Sheriff Clark."

"Let me call back for him." The woman's voice came out all girly. When I'd asked her a simple question the last time I was there, she could barely look up from her phone to answer me. "He will be right out. Is there anything I can get you?"

"No," John said. "We're fine." He guided me to a seat in the waiting room. We sat down next to each other, and he gripped my hand. "You looked so scared that day I picked you up from here."

"I was being accused of murder. And that woman wasn't as nice to me as she was to you."

John chuckled. "You almost sound jealous."

"I'm not jealous."

He squeezed my hand. "You have nothing to worry about, Beautiful."

The door to the back swung open, and the sheriff walked out. "Thank you for coming down. Let's go back to my office."

Once again, the walk through the back area was the same. The room was full of deputies watching each step I took. A few turned and whispered to each other. My feet stopped a few steps outside the sheriff's office door. I could see Nate sitting in the chair. His shaggy blond hair was tousled, and he was wearing one of his signature polos with jeans.

No matter how angry I was at him, I couldn't hold the happy tears back for seeing my friend again. I rushed into the room, and Nate jumped up from the chair and wrapped his arms around me. It wasn't until I heard someone clear their throat that I noticed Pedro was in the room. I dropped my arms from Nate and stepped back.

Pedro stood up and held out his hand. "It's good to see you, Annabella."

I grabbed his hand and shook it. "I'm so happy you guys are okay. Nate, I would like you to meet John."

John held out his hand and wrapped his other arm around my waist. "Nice to meet you, Nate."

Nate raised his eyebrow at John's hand. "Looks like I missed some news."

I grinned shyly. "Let's talk later."

Everyone sat down.

"Ms. Harper, we are sorry for the accusations and what we, the department, put you through. Here is your passport." The sheriff turned toward Nate. "Now, can you explain where you've been for the last week?"

Nate shifted in his seat, and Pedro grabbed his hand. "It wasn't Nate's fault. It is all a funny story. I accidentally cut my hand on a knife at Nate's house, and Nate here rushed me to the ER. If you call Los Angeles Community Hospital, they have records of me coming in."

I glanced at John, and he shook his head.

Pedro continued his story. "After my hand was fixed, I begged Nate to go to our house up in Santa Clarita for a few days. We needed time to ourselves. He had been so busy at work. We turned off our phones and the TV and spent a few days vegging out. When we turned on the TV yesterday and noticed the reports, we called Annabella immediately."

"This is the story you're going with?" the sheriff asked. "You cost the department a lot of money."

I shifted in my seat. John placed a hand over his mouth. I could tell he was trying not to laugh. The sheriff's eyes were locked on Nate and Pedro, and they both shifted in their seats.

Sheriff Clark tapped his pen on the desk before he leaned back. "You know I'm going to have to charge you with obstruction of justice."

"Will he have to go to jail?" I asked.

The sheriff couldn't hold his composure anymore. "Brock called me this morning and let me know what was found. I have to admit Nate you told a good story."

"But now the mafia is going to come after Pedro and me. Hell they might come after Marta again. We promised not to tell them they were behind it."

"The evidence Neal and John's sister pulled was done illegally. I can't use any of the information against the mob. Most everything they pulled, we already know about. You still need to pay for the man hours we used to find you."

"I can do that with an additional donation to the sheriff's office," Nate said in relief. "Thank you for everything. Can we go now?"

John shifted forward in his chair. "I have one further question. Who kept calling and pushing the accusation that Annabella was guilty?"

Sheriff Clark scratched his beard. "Brock asked the same question. We kept getting tons of anonymous calls. Then people started calling and telling us all these things she had done. Sorry, Annabella, but you sounded like a bitch. Brock and I talked most of the stuff out. It seemed someone has been watching you. When Nate left town after being beaten up, whoever this is used the opportunity to pin the murder on you."

John stood and shook the sheriff's hand. "We'll be in touch." When I stood up, he placed his hand at the base of my back and guided me out of the room.

The sheriff nodded as everyone left the room.

Nate stopped me when we exited the building. "Bella." Usually, I would forgive him in a second, but I wasn't ready to forgive him.

"No, Nate. I'm not ready. My stuff will be moved out

of the house as soon as I find something, and for right now, I'm staying with Daisy."

He took a step forward, and I held up my hand. "Nate, I'm not ready yet. Give me time. I was excited to see you were okay, but you let me take the fall for murder." I turned and walked toward the car. I wasn't in the mood to listen to his sob story. Someone was still out there, waiting for me.

John placed his hand on my back. He didn't say anything. He was just there for me, and I was about to lose him. He had no reason to stay in California, other than my car issue that Neal said he was looking into.

When we both got into the SUV, it was silent. I could feel the tension. Neither one of us wanted to ask what was next, but one of us needed to. "John, what are we doing?"

He pushed the start button on the SUV and grabbed the steering wheel. "Lunch."

"Lunch?"

"You never make decisions on an empty stomach, so where do you want to go get lunch?" He backed out of the parking lot and headed toward Rodeo Drive. I told him I wanted to hit one of the new farm-to-table restaurants. Neither of us spoke during the short drive to the restaurant.

When we sat down, John ordered a scotch. I took his lead and ordered a margarita. "Are we going to keep putting off the conversation?"

He leaned back in the chair. His black T-shirt stretched across his chest. He had his dark aviator glasses on, the same ones he'd worn on the day he picked me up from the station. I couldn't see his eyes. I had no clue what he was thinking.

When he didn't answer my question, I tapped my finger on the edge of my glass. "When are you leaving?"

John let out a sigh. "Brock needs me to head out of the country on a mission. I don't know when yet."

"Oh."

He reached across the table and grabbed my hand. "Do you want me to come back?" John tugged my lip from my teeth. "I want to come back, but I also need to do my job. I want this to work. Do you?"

I let out the breath I was holding. "Yes. I just don't know."

The waitress used that moment to come back to the table. John and I both ended up ordering the daily special. Once we ordered, the waitress left.

"How do you see us making this work?" I asked. "My life is here, and yours is in Ft. Lauderdale."

"Do you trust me?"

"Yes." I didn't even have to think about my answer.

John took a sip of his scotch. "Then we have nothing to worry about. I plan to stay another week and make sure we figure out who put the bomb in the car. In the beginning of this, we'll fly back and forth. Maybe in the future, I can work from California."

"But all of your friends are in Ft. Lauderdale."

John looked off into the distance then took his sunglasses off. I was lost in his gray eyes. "Yes. My friends are in Ft. Lauderdale, but you're out here, and I want to be with you. So let's take this one day at a time and see how things go."

I felt like the weight of the world had been lifted off my shoulders.

John's phone vibrated on the table. His sister's name flashed across the screen. Over the past couple of days, I had talked to her more. John had told me about her looking for their mom.

"I will call her later," he said. "This is our time." His phone started to ring again, and he pushed the silence button. Then Addie called a third time.

He reached for it and swiped across the screen. "Hey, pip-squeak. I'm kind of busy."

His brow furrowed as she spoke.

"Are you sure?" John ran his hand through his hair and let out a deep breath. "I can't leave here. Annabella needs me. We don't know who's after her." I could only hear one side of the conversation, but it sounded like his sister needed him. I wasn't about to stand in her way.

"Let me talk to Annabella, and I will call you back."

John hung up the phone. "When do you have to be back on set?"

The movie *Last Love* had already been delayed a week because of me. Each day we weren't shooting cost the film more money. "I planned to go back tomorrow. Tell me what's going on."

"Addie found our mom." John's voice cracked.

"You need to go."

He took another swig of his scotch. "We don't know who's after you. I can't leave."

"Nobody's done anything in a few days. I can hire Gabriel as my bodyguard until we figure out what's going on, or I can hire someone else."

John pushed his plate to the side. "I haven't seen my mom in years. I'm not one hundred percent convinced it's her. I can stay here a few more days."

"You need to go and be with your sister. I promise to be safe. I'm going to spend hours on set."

"I will be back in a couple days, and then we can figure everything out."

"When do you have to leave?" I knew it would be soon, and I wanted him to go be with family, but selfishly, I didn't want him to leave.

"Addie booked me on the next flight out. I leave in two hours."

14

ANNABELLA

My alarm echoed through the large bedroom at Daisy's house. I was used to living in enormous homes since I'd made it in Hollywood. Some days, I still missed the small one-bedroom my mom had raised me in. I could've fit that whole apartment in my current bedroom. Sadness washed over me as I thought about my mother. She'd died of breast cancer the year I graduated from high school. With her agoraphobia, she wouldn't leave the house to get treatment, and we couldn't afford to have a nurse come to the house.

I slowly woke up and stretched my legs out before getting out of bed. I turned to look at the clock on the end table. *Five-thirty.* This was my first day back on set, my first return to my normal life. I wasn't ready to go back. I wanted to jump on a plane and go see John.

We'd texted last night before I fell asleep. I reached for my phone and saw I had a missed text from John.

John: *Good luck on your first day back. Text me when you are done, Beautiful.*

I couldn't help but scroll back over the conversation we'd had the night before. He was so sweet and considerate. He cared more about my safety and me going back to work than about meeting his mom. His flight hadn't gotten in until well after midnight. He was going to his sister's house this morning for breakfast and to find out what was going on. He would be heading over there soon.

Annabella: *Text me how it goes. I want to know everything.*

The three little dots came up on the screen. My heart picked up as I waited to see what he would write. I had never been with anyone that made me sit and watch the three dots, waiting to see what they would write. I had already opened my heart to him in a short time.

John and I clicked. My fame didn't seem to bother him. I liked how he wanted to stay in and just be with me. He didn't care about going to the new local restaurant or hot spot to be caught on camera by the paparazzi. When I'd tried to pay for breakfast the other day, he'd almost seemed appalled. Men in my past had never tried to pay. Now I understood how Daisy felt with Neal and Aaron. John was a good guy.

I glanced at the clock on my phone. I needed to get my ass in gear. I showered and changed into casual clothes. I would spend a few hours in hair and makeup before I was on set. *Last Love* only had four more days of filming before it wrapped. The director had worked on filming all the scenes without me, and all that was left were my scenes.

I couldn't wait for *Last Love* to come out. I knew it would be another blockbuster hit. My next film started filming next week. When the contracts came in, I had given myself two weeks off between films. But *Last Love* had started shooting late, and I'd taken a week off because of Nate. Now I only had two days off before I started the next movie. Filming for *Breaking Hearts* would take three months to shoot. I didn't know when I would get to see John again.

When I was ready, I went downstairs and grabbed a muffin from the kitchen before I headed to the studio.

Gabriel stood at the counter, sipping from a mug of coffee. "Ready?"

I nodded. It would be strange to bring a bodyguard along on the job. Plus Gabriel was on the quiet side. I had offered to take him out for dinner to thank him for saving me, but he'd said it was part of his job.

We headed toward the set. My car was getting fixed, so we took the rented SUV. Now Gabriel did a sweep of the SUV before we got in each time. Nobody had tried anything since the bomb. I was hoping the person forgot about me and went away. Or it was the mob, and they no longer wanted to come after me.

I waved hello to Jeremy, the man who worked the gates to the set. He hit the button for us to come in. Gabriel drove us to the back of the set, near the stage for *Last Love*.

Three people stood next to my trailer—my manager, assistant, and producer. I hadn't thought about how things would go today. I wasn't sure I was ready to talk about any of it. I had talked to my manager a couple of times, but Roxy, my assistant for this movie, and I hadn't talked much.

Some days I wondered why I kept her on my staff. I didn't use her—I just did things myself.

"You sure you're ready for this?" Gabriel asked.

"No, but it's my job." I grabbed the handle to the SUV and jumped out of the car.

Roxy ran up and gave me a hug. "We've missed you so much. Did someone really try to kill you with a bomb? And there's a rumor you called off the wedding. Does that mean Nate is single? What was it like when you were taken in for questioning?"

Her rapid-fire questions surprised me. "I don't really want to talk about it. Can you get a hold of my realtor and have her meet me here on my lunch break?"

"My cousin is a good realtor," the young girl replied as she bounced on her toes.

I hated firing people because I knew what it was like to be looking for a job and hoping food would be on the table the next day. But she was acting inappropriate. Luckily, we only had four days left on the movie. "Please call my realtor. Thank you."

Needing space, I turned and headed for my trailer. Marcus, my manager, and Lucas, the producer, stepped in my path. "Please let me get ready. I'm here to work not gab."

Marcus frowned at my comment, and Lucas nodded before he turned and walked toward the set.

I reached for the handle on my trailer when Gabriel nudged me out of the way. "Let me look first."

I couldn't help but roll my eyes. I stepped to the side and let Gabriel into my trailer. I looked down at my phone and scrolled back to the conversation with John. It was easier for me to ask questions about the BDSM lifestyle in a text rather than face-to-face. We had talked in depth about the lifestyle, and the more I researched, the more I wanted to open myself to that part of John's world.

The sound of Gabriel flinging the door to the trailer open startled me. He jumped out, slammed the door shut, and pressed his phone to his ear. "You can't go in there."

I grabbed Gabriel's shirt as he started to walk by me. "What happened?"

Gabriel glanced back at the trailer. "Annabella, you

don't need to worry about it. I will take care of everything. Stay right here and don't move. Set security is standing over there." He pointed at the building. Two men dressed in black suits stood next to the doors. "If you see anything out of the ordinary, scream. I need to grab something out of the SUV." Gabriel turned and jogged toward the SUV.

What could be so bad that I couldn't go into the trailer? Was there another dead body? I needed to see. Gabriel had his back turned to me when I opened the door and went in. I walked two feet and immediately regretted my decision. I counted six rattlesnakes spread out around the trailer. The one closest moved toward me. I scrambled for the door handle, but when I went to open it, it wouldn't budge.

I turned and pounded on the door. I heard Gabriel cuss on the other side. With both hands, I tugged on the door handle, but it wouldn't move. I was trapped. I glanced back over my shoulder and saw the closest snake coiled into his attack position. His tail rattled before he lunged forward. I jumped, and he missed me by a centimeter. Before he could attack again, I climbed to the top of the kitchen counter next to the door.

The counter was out of reach for the snakes. My only saving grace was that the snakes were babies, only a foot long. If they were full-grown, they would have been able to strike up the side of the cabinet. But I got a better look around my trailer. It wasn't only six snakes—there were more than I could count. My phone vibrated in my hand. John's name flashed across the screen.

I swiped it with a shaky finger. "Hi, John."

His voice came through panicked. "Are you okay?"

"Yep, just sitting on the counter in my trailer."

He let out a sigh. "Jesus, Annabella, there are deadly snakes in your trailer, and Gabriel can't get back in. He went to get a crowbar. What were you thinking, going in there after he said to stay out?"

Anger bubbled up. I didn't like being told what to do. "Well, if he would have said 'your trailer's covered in snakes,' I would've. But he said to stay out, and I wanted to know what happened. My first thought was that there was a dead body or Nate's body." I took a deep breath. "Sorry." I couldn't hold back the tears. I wanted John, and he was on the other side of the country.

His voice softened. "I didn't mean to yell. It's hard being this far away. I'm going to try to find a flight out today."

The selfish side of me wanted him to come and see me. But I knew Gabriel could protect me if I listened, and John needed to spend time with his family.

"No. You need to stay with your family. Talk to me until they can get me out of here." Another snaked hissed. They were coming from every direction. Luckily, none of them seemed tempted to climb up the cabinet. I could hear the pounding outside the door as Gabriel tried to get in.

"It's really her," John said.

My heart cracked at the sadness in his voice. "Did you ask where she's been?"

He let out another sigh. "She said our father was too much, so she left and started over."

What kind of woman could leave her two kids? "I'm sorry."

"I'm going to catch the first flight out tomorrow and head back to you. I'll let my mom finish telling her side of the story today. But I need time to process what she's said so far."

After another pound on the door, I could see daylight through the cracks. Gabriel hit it two more times, and the door flew open. I screamed as the snake closest to the door lunged at Gabriel. He jumped to the side, and the snake slithered across the pavement outside. I heard a few screams as people rushed away.

Gabriel reached for me. "On the count of three, jump into my arms."

He barely got to three before I jumped off the counter and into his arms. He yanked me outside of the trailer, and a man wearing a security T-shirt slammed the door behind us. I let out a sigh of relief. Gabriel's lips flattened, and his eyes tightened. Extras and workers on the film stood in the distance, watching what was going on.

"John, I'm out of the trailer and safe," I said into the phone. "I need to head into makeup. I promise to call you at lunch."

"Be safe, Beautiful, and don't let Gabriel out of your sight."

That morning, I would have scoffed at the demand. But I knew I needed to stay close. I hung up the phone and watched Gabriel as he worked to remove the snakes from my trailer. The director stood by the set entrance, waving me over to makeup. Gabriel was next to me as I walked toward makeup. He hadn't said a word, but his jaw ticked. He didn't leave my side as I sat through two hours of makeup.

I sent John a quick text letting him know I was still okay and heading to set. By the time I was done with makeup and wardrobe, it was close to ten o'clock. We were shooting a scene in which I was running through the streets of Manhattan. It was all done in front of a green screen. Everything went as planned, and we finished up the morning shoot by one o'clock. My stomach growled.

I sat down at a table in the dining area with a pasta salad and sandwich. Gabriel sat across from me. "Sorry," I mumbled between bites of my turkey sandwich.

He pinched the bridge of his nose. "Do you know how worried I was when you went in there? I didn't say 'stay out' for fun, Annabella. John put his trust in me to keep you safe, and I already failed."

"You didn't fail. I didn't listen, and you got me out with no problem." It had been stupid of me to go in there. I took a bite of my pasta salad and froze. I spit the salad out but knew it was too late. I could feel my tongue start to swell. "My purse," I choked out.

Gabriel sprinted back toward the SUV. I hoped he would make it back in time.

Someone had put seafood in the salad. The set had been explicitly told no shellfish since I was allergic.

15

JOHN

When Gabriel called and told me about Annabella's allergic reaction to seafood, I booked a flight back. Someone was trying to kill her, and I wasn't about to stay in Boston another minute. Annabella didn't know I was coming back. Addie understood why I was leaving.

My mom gave me an awkward hug when I walked out the door. She had never left the house when we were growing up, yet she'd changed her name, moved to another state, and started another family. Addie's source had found her, and our mom had come to talk before her new family found out about us.

I called Annabella when I was on my way to the airport. I didn't tell her I was coming. She refused to go back to Daisy's house. She was worried she would put them in danger. So Gabriel took her to a hotel near the studio. He added me to the room so I could grab a key and head up when I got there. Addie had booked a suite, and Gabriel was staying in one of the rooms.

It was two o'clock in the morning when I arrived. I grabbed the key from the front desk and went to the top floor of the hotel. The door opened with ease, and I set my bag on the floor. Gabriel was on the couch and nodded toward Annabella's room.

I walked into her room and discarded my shirt and jeans. Annabella turned over on her back. Her tight white tank top stretched across her luscious breasts. The moonlight shed enough light for me to see her nipples through the thin material.

"John?" In two giant strides, I was next to the bed. Annabella sat up and threw herself at me. I caught her in midair. A sob broke from the back of her throat. "Someone's trying to kill me."

My throat tightened at how close they had come today when she'd eaten the seafood. If Gabriel hadn't acted as fast as he had, she would be dead, and whoever was doing this would have won.

I pulled her in closer. Her tears dripped onto my shoulder. Annabella shook in my arms. I didn't regret my decision to leave Boston and come back to check on her. Having her in my arms was all I needed to know that she needed me as much as I needed her. I had been in pure terror when I found out what had happened.

Leaning back so I could see her pretty green eyes, I wiped the tears from her face. "I will make sure nothing happens to you."

"You can't." Sobs punctuated her words. "You have to go to work."

I gently pushed her onto her back. "Brock understands. We have other people who can go on the missions. I'm not leaving your side until we find out what is going on."

"But you'll have to leave sometime." Her lip trembled as she spoke.

I ran my hands down her arms and gently pushed her back so she was lying down. Annabella's blond hair covered the pillow like a halo. Her breath hitched as I ran kisses down the side of her neck. I wanted to take her mind off of what had happened the day before.

"I need you, John," she whispered.

I slowly ran my finger along her tight stomach, pushing her white tank top up as I went. Her nipples poked through the thin material, begging to be touched. Gently pulling her tank top over her breasts, I leaned down and took her nipple into my mouth.

Her breath hitched as I sucked. Her hand came up, and she ran her fingers through my hair. "More," she moaned.

I gently bit down on her nipple, and her hips came

off the bed. She moaned louder as I switched to the other nipple.

I let go of her nub. "I missed you so much." I had been gone a day, but it felt like a week. I didn't know what I would do when I had to go on week-long missions. But I couldn't think about that now.

"I missed you too. Please, I need you inside me."

I tweaked her nipple. "So demanding. I think I'm going to spend some time worshipping your body."

The night before, Annabella had started to ask me questions about the BDSM lifestyle. I hadn't been able to hold back the smile when she'd asked if I would spank her when she didn't do what I wanted. Since leaving the Navy, I hadn't had sex outside of Club Sanctorum until Annabella. If she'd asked me to walk away from the lifestyle, I would have. But after our conversation, I knew she was curious, and I planned to slowly bring BDSM aspects into our lovemaking.

I leaned down and kissed her breast. Her breath hitched each time my lips touched her skin. "Have you come up with a safe word like we talked about?"

Her body stilled under me. "Can we do the stop lights like you talked about? Red, green, and yellow?" Her question came out rushed.

I rolled to the side so I could see her pretty green eyes. While I talked, I continued to run my hands over her breasts. "If you're nervous, we don't need to do anything."

"I want to. I want to be in this part of your life. I'm scared."

I brushed the blond lock off her forehead. "If anything scares you or you want to stop and ask more questions, say 'yellow,' okay?" Annabella nodded. "I need to hear you say yes."

"Yes. I will say yellow. I have another question." Her eyes darted around the room nervously.

I liked her. There was no question she could ask that would change how I felt. Whenever she walked into a room, my dick got hard, and everything around us went away. "Ask any question you want."

"The other day when I accidentally walked in on Aaron and Daisy, she called him master. Am I supposed to be calling you master?"

In the club, I always required the subs to call me sir. Daisy had called me master for a while, but it had never felt right to me. The other night when I made love to Annabella, I'd loved the sound of her saying my name as she went over the edge.

"No. You can say my name."

Her pretty little lips turned down, and she looked away.

"Talk to me, Annabella. I can't read your mind."

"But Daisy said you would want me to call you sir or master. Does this mean you really don't want me to be in that part of your life? Will you still go to the club and be with another woman?"

I gently gripped her chin and turned her face toward me. "I'm with you, Annabella, no other woman. And I would hope you don't plan on sleeping with another man. As for the master or sir, I like the way my name sounds on your lips. That isn't saying in the future, or when we go to Club Sanctorum, I won't ask you to call me sir or master. But this is us, and we can figure it out as we go. We don't need to set all the rules of our relationship tonight."

ANNABELLA

Each time John ran his hand down my side, my breath hitched. My heart was beating a mile a minute. We had made love a few times, but this seemed different. I needed him more than I need my next breath.

When the door to the bedroom had opened earlier, fear had washed over me until I saw John's face in the moonlight. I didn't know it was possible to fall for a man so quickly, but him coming when I needed him meant the world to me.

"I will be right back, Beautiful." John jumped off the bed and dug through my suitcase. When he lay back down next to me, he had one of the scarfs I'd brought along. "Let me see your wrists." When I held them out to him, he gently tied the scarf around them and placed my hands above my head. My heart felt like it was about to beat out of my chest. "Don't move your hands. Each time you move, I will stop. If you keep your hands above your head, I will bring you to orgasm."

He moved so he was kneeling between my legs. I wanted to reach out and run my hands down his chest, but I stopped myself and moved them behind my head instead. John's mouth twitched. He knew how hard this was for me. I loved running my hands all over his body.

John pulled my tank top up my body and bunched it over my eyes. The tank top also kept my arms in place above my head. "Just feel, Beautiful."

When John's lips wrapped around my nipple, my body arched off the bed. It felt more intense than it had a few minutes ago when he'd had his lips on me. His hands worked my boy shorts down my body. Then he shifted, and his lips left my body. "God. Fucking beautiful."

I didn't have a chance to respond before his lips touched my clit.

"So wet," he mumbled as he licked my pearl.

My body ached for more contact. I wanted him to slip inside me. I needed to feel him closer.

"Stay still," he commanded.

I fought the urge to lift my hips for more friction. My body felt like it was on fire. It was so hard to stay still. A whimper left my mouth. John's words from earlier rang in my head. He would stop if I moved my hands. But if I stayed still, he would give me an orgasm.

"Please."

John bit down on my nub and slipped a finger into my velvety folds. The little bit of pain mixed with the pleasure from his tongue was enough to send me over the edge. My body arched, and I screamed out his name as he continued to lick and touch me.

"Perfect. You are so beautiful when you come."

I could feel my face redden at his words. Whenever John talked about how beautiful I was, it felt genuine. I knew he meant it, unlike the rest of the world.

"I hope you're comfortable, Beautiful. I'm not done yet and plan to spend some more time down here." John positioned my knees over his wide shoulders and levered one arm under my butt. He leaned down and slowly licked my clit.

I couldn't believe how close he had me to the edge again. Each time I was about to go over, he would pull back and kiss my inner thigh. Then when my body started to come back down, he would bring me back to the edge again.

"I can't take any more, John. I need you." I whimpered when I felt his tongue leave my body.

"You've been perfect, keeping your arms up." John leaned forward, and I felt the scarf fall from my arms. He slowly worked the tank top the rest of the way up my arms. Then he leaned down and licked my lips before he pressed his to mine. The kiss was gentle and full of need.

I wrapped my legs around his waist and lifted my hips to get some relief. John pulled back farther. I could feel him smile against my lips. "Condom," he said before he pulled away and grabbed his jeans off the floor. I had completely forgotten about everything except my need for him.

He ripped the wrapping with his teeth, and I watched as he sheathed himself. My fingers itched to reach out and grab his member. When he had the condom rolled down his length, he leaned over me and pressed his lips to mine.

John kept his eyes open as he gently pushed into me. He clenched his jaw, and I leaned forward and ran kisses down his neck. I was moaning and squirming by the time he was entirely inside of me. Then he stopped.

I tried to buck up against him to get him to move. "Please."

"You feel so good," John ground out before he leaned down and kissed my lips.

Once he started to move, I held on to him tightly. He began to thrust hard, and when he reached his hand between us and pinched my nub, my hips left the bed, and I screamed his name. John picked up the speed, and he wasn't far behind me when I felt him let go. His body slumped, and he used his forearms to keep his weight off of me.

He leaned down and kissed my nose. "I will be right back." John left the bed to dispose of the condom in the bathroom. His tight ass flexed with each step. I couldn't believe how lucky I was. Maybe one day I would forgive Nate because being accused of his murder had brought me closer to John.

John slid into the bed next to me. "What are you thinking about, Beautiful?"

"I'm glad I got accused of murder." John's eyes widened. I couldn't help but laugh and snuggle in closer. "I wouldn't have found you if Nate didn't cause all these issues."

"I would rather have met you at Daisy's party. I'm just glad I'm in your life. Now we need to figure out who is still after you."

Tonight, I would lie in the arms of the man I was falling for, and tomorrow I would worry about who was trying to kill me.

16

ANNABELLA

I lay in bed, not believing how lucky I was to have found someone who cared about me. John shifted beside me. I rolled over on my side to watch him sleep, but he was already up. His eyes were full of desire. When he went to give me a kiss, my phone rang on the nightstand.

I reached over to grab it and saw my manager's name flashing across the screen. "Yes, Marcus," I answered.

"You need to be on set. The director said if we stop anymore, you'll be cut."

John reached out to pull me back into bed. I quickly ducked and made my way to the bathroom. I didn't want to be cut from the film. I knew they wouldn't cut me because they didn't have time to find anyone else. The director just needed someone to yell at, and it was me.

"I'm getting ready. I will be to set on time."

My manager hadn't handled the press or the director well. Instead of getting out and trying to clear my name, he'd stayed quiet. He hadn't even called to see how I was doing. I'd called the producers of *Last Love* directly to let them know I had been accused of murder.

An hour later, I was back on set. I couldn't help but feeling that someone was watching me. John stood next to my chair. His eyes were hidden behind his aviator glasses. I couldn't help the groan I let out as Roxy, my assistant on set, headed our way.

"Annabella, I had your realtor scheduled to show up yesterday, and then you disappeared. You made me look bad."

"Someone put seafood on the lunch menu, and I had an allergic reaction. Filming was canceled after lunch. It's your job to make sure I have what I need, and you also have a list of my allergies. Why didn't you let me know?"

The young girl rolled her eyes. "I don't have time to check the lunch menu for you. Shouldn't you check what's in the food before you shovel it into your mouth?"

I glanced at John. He shook his head, and I could

tell he was about to open his mouth. I decided to address the matter before he could. "Roxy, it seems the job of being my assistant on set is too hard. You're fired. I don't need your help anymore."

"You can't fire me."

Director Paterson looked up from the script. "Actually, she can. You're supposed to work for her."

John motioned for security to come over. Two men in black shirts walked over and escorted the young girl out. My assistant's job was to make mine easier on set. One of the main things she was in charge of was food. The job description stated she was to make sure no seafood was on set, and if there was, she was supposed to order me a different lunch.

The rest of the morning passed with no more issues. John worked as my assistant for the rest of the day. He had water waiting for me when I finished a scene. When it came time to eat lunch, he had my favorite burger place bring in food. Well, he sent Gabriel to go grab our food.

I had two scenes left, and then I would be done filming the movie. I couldn't wait to be done. Nothing but bad things had happened in my life since filming had started. The stage crew was working on getting the stage set for the next scene.

I hopped up from my chair. "I'm going to run to the bathroom."

John got up from the chair next to me.

I put my hand on his arm. "Stay." When it looked like he was about to protest, I said, "I'm running to the bathroom. It will be fine. I promise."

He grabbed my arm and pulled me back into his then placed a kiss on my lips. "Five minutes."

The bathroom was on the other side of the studio. It would take me almost five minutes to get there. But there was no point in arguing with the man. I turned and walked toward the back of the studio and waved at the two men working on the set.

My next scene would mostly be done in front of the green screen again. I was being pushed off a building in the next scene. I was going to have to climb up on the platform they'd built and fall off. The first time I'd done the stunt had been scary, but they had strapped me into a harness, and I'd fallen onto a soft mat.

I rounded the corner and came face-to-face with my manager. He stepped in front of me, blocking my path. "Annabella, we need to talk." The pudgy old man had been my manager since I'd gotten my first gig. Most movies came to me, so he didn't have to do much except collect a check. It was probably time for me to find a more motivated manager.

I tried to step around him. "I need to go to the bathroom."

"I didn't want to do this. But she has so much power."

"Who?" I asked, confused. Two seconds later, I felt the metal jab into my side.

"Don't scream, bitch."

With each step, I tried to struggle out of the person's grasp. My hand shot up and tried to pry the fingers away from my mouth. The grip was so tight, I could feel my skin bruise under the pressure.

The emergency exit door flew open, and another man stood there. He was at least six feet tall, dressed in black, and wearing a black ski mask. He grabbed my free arm.

It was hard to fight back. I even tried to make my body limp, but the two men were strong and pulled me along. The bright sun blinded me for a second when I was shoved outside.

An Aston Martin Vantage sat with the trunk open outside the door. My capturer released his hand from my mouth for a second, and I used the opportunity to scream for help. The second man slapped me so hard across the face that my vision faded to black for a moment.

Within seconds, they shoved me into the trunk of the car and slammed it shut. I reached up and touched my cheek. It throbbed with pain. The car squealed out of the parking lot. With each turn and bump it made, my body was thrown against the side of the trunk. The warm California sun heated up the containment space, and sweat beaded down my face and back. I looked for some way to escape.

Even if I could find a way out of the car, it felt like it was speeding down the highway, farther and farther from the man I wanted to spend the rest of my life with. The car came to an abrupt stop, and I flew against the back. My forehead hit the metal arms of the trunk, and I felt blood trickle down my forehead.

Does John even know I'm gone yet? I wondered how far these men would make it with me before he could figure out what was going on. I shivered. A feeling of dread came over me.

The voices from inside the car were muffled. I strained to hear what they were saying. The two men started to argue, but with the music on, it was hard to understand them. Before I could figure it out, the car took off again, making my body fly against the side. The carpet skinned my elbows as I tried to stay in place.

In one of the action movies I'd played in, they had put me in the back of the car. I had acted like I knew exactly where I would be when I came out by counting turns. In reality, I'd lost track of everything once we had turned left out of the studio parking lot.

It felt like I had been in the trunk for hours when the car finally came to a stop and I heard the two car doors open and close. I pulled my arm back, trying to get leverage so I could punch whoever opened the trunk. My only option was to try to get free and run.

The trunk door popped open, and I began kicking and punching. My hand collided with one of the kidnapper's faces. He grunted and hit back. My head snapped when his fist connected with my jaw. A metallic taste filled my mouth. He grabbed me by the hair and dragged me out of the car. Then he threw me to the hard pavement and kicked my side. I felt my ribs crack when his foot connected.

"Stop," someone yelled.

I opened my eyes to see a woman standing on the stairs. She was wearing an elegant red dress. Her brown hair was curled, and she wore lipstick that matched her ruby-red dress.

"Bring her into the house."

The two men grabbed me under the arms and dragged me toward the house. I tried to get my feet under me and keep up, but my knees scraped along the cement. Each man had such a firm grip on my arms, it felt like they would break them in two.

I tried to remember where I had seen the woman before. Even the house I was dragged through seemed like something I had seen on TV before. But I couldn't place the woman or the house. Maybe if my body wasn't in so much pain, I could concentrate and figure out what was going on.

My vision went out for a second. When I came back, I was strapped to a chair in a large office. Old books lined the walls. A large dark oak desk sat in front of me, and the woman from earlier sat behind it.

"Nice of you to finally wake up, Annabella," she said.

"Sorry that me being beaten took time out of your day." I didn't see the blow coming from the left until it was too late.

"Jeremy, stop hitting her. I need her awake for this. When I'm done, I don't care what you do with her."

"It seems you know my name, and I don't know yours."

Her cold glare sent a shiver of fear down my spine. The man who kept hitting me smiled. But it wasn't a smile that put me at ease. It made me scared of what he would do to me.

"I guess it doesn't matter if you know my name. You won't live to tell anyone what I did. My name is Isabella." The name and her face seemed so familiar, but I couldn't get the fog to leave my brain.

When I looked back at the woman behind the desk, the picture above her caught my attention. Once I saw the man she stood next to in the photograph, it clicked into place who she was, but I still didn't understand why she'd had me beaten. I would bet she was also behind the few attempts on my life.

"Wh-what do you want?" I asked.

"For being a dumb movie-star blonde, you sure do know how to escape death. But you aren't going to live through today."

I swallowed past the lump in my throat. When I ran my tongue across my teeth, I tasted blood. "Why are you trying to kill me?"

"Like you don't know." Her words were laced with hatred. "Did you think you could get money out of us?"

"Money? Why would I want your money?" I tried to raise my hand to protect myself from another blow to the face, but my hands wouldn't move since they were tied to the chair. The impact hurt just as badly as the last one had. It was getting harder to keep my eyes open. One was already swollen shut from being punched.

"I know you didn't ask for money yet. Maybe you're planning on going to the media with the story."

I squinted my one good eye, trying to figure out what the hell this woman was talking about. "I don't need your money. I'm in the press enough. Why do you think I want or need anything from your people?"

I should've asked John to come to the bathroom with me. I could tell he'd struggled with the decision to let me go alone. Now he would never forgive himself for my death. I knew it would be coming soon. The woman in front of me may have been liked by the public, but she looked crazy. She wouldn't get her hands dirty. The men next to me would be the ones to kill me. I just wanted to know why I was about to die.

The woman stood, placed her hands on the wood desk, and leaned forward. "You don't have to act dumb. Your lawyer confirmed you received the DNA test and the letter from us."

I closed my eye and let my head fall back. Nate and I had done that crazy DNA test together. He'd wanted to help me find my birth father even though I wasn't sure if I was ready. We'd done the test and had the results sent to his law office. I remembered seeing the test on the counter at the house, but I'd never thought anything about it.

"Are you saying that Governor Jackson is my father?"

"Like you didn't know. You had your lawyer contact us for a meet and greet. Luckily, I intercepted the call before my do-gooder husband heard about it. He would want to do right by you. You know what this scandal will do to his career?"

Scandal. Career. This was all too much. "I don't want anything."

The woman huffed and threw up her hands. "I can't take the chance. My husband plans to run against Zack Turner. I can't have this scandal sitting out here if he plans to win."

My time was running out. The woman really thought I would ruin her husband's chance of running for president. It was only a matter of time before she would kill me.

She looked at the man next to me. "Take her away and make sure you kill her this time."

The guy to my left punched me again, and this time, the room went dark. I was going to die.

17

JOHN

"Did you happen to see Annabella on your way over here?" I asked Gabriel.

He shook his head. "No. There was no one back there, and most of the lights were off. Are you sure she went back that way?"

"She ran to the bathroom, but she's been gone six minutes."

"Maybe she went to another one. Are you positive she went to the one over there?" He pointed in the direction Annabella had gone.

"Yes." I jumped out of my chair and ran toward the ladies' room. I could hear Gabriel behind me. I threw the door to the women's room open and pushed open each stall door. She wasn't there. "Fuck."

I grabbed the phone out of my pocket and called Brock. He answered on the first ring. "Hey, John."

"Can you hack the cameras at Annabella's work?"

I could already hear his fingers hitting the keyboard. "You want me to hack Universal Studios' cameras?"

"Yes. Is that possible?" I started to walk back toward the director's chair. He would need to know what was going on.

The director was in a conversation with Annabella's manager.

"Annabella is missing," I said. "We need to lock down the area."

The manager started to puff out his chest. "You can't just go around demanding things of the director. Annabella is a diva. Are you sure she didn't just get sick of you and go home for the day?" I couldn't believe she paid this douchebag a dime.

The director turned from Annabella's manager to me. "She wouldn't just disappear, and I don't know why you think she's a diva. You've been trying to get me to drop her from the film since she got arrested for murder. You're supposed to work for your client, not against them."

"Thanks, Director Paterson," I said. "I've got someone looking at the camera feed right now."

"I'm not going to even ask how that's possible," Director Paterson said.

Marcus became pale. "You can't do that."

I raised an eyebrow, and my phone rang a second later. "Hey," I answered.

"You might want to find Annabella's manager." I looked around the room and saw the fucker heading for the door. "Gabriel, grab him."

Gabriel took off at a full sprint toward the man.

"What did you see, Brock?" I could hear someone else in the room with Brock. It sounded like his wife, Jessica.

"She talked to her agent for a few seconds before a man in a black mask came up behind her and put a gun to her back. They took her outside and pushed her into the trunk of her manager's car."

My stomach dropped. How far could they have gotten? Who the hell was after her?

Gabriel walked back in with Annabella's manager. Her manager was threatening to sue Gabriel for manhandling him. I didn't care what Gabriel did as long as we could figure out who the fuck was after Annabella. Gabriel pushed the pudgy guy into the director's chair. When he tried to stand, Gabriel pushed him back down.

"Sit," Gabriel demanded.

"I have a video of you helping a man kidnap Annabella," I said. "Who has her, and why?"

"I can't tell you." Her manager was a short, fat guy. He started to cry when I leaned in farther. "She has so much power. She said she would ruin me if I didn't help her."

"If I leak that video to the press, your career is over. How do you think it looks to let your biggest client get kidnapped?" I paced in front of the director's chair. "If you don't give me a name within the next few minutes, I'm sending the video to the press and making sure you're never hired by anyone else, you sniveling piece of shit."

I wanted this man to pay for the pain I knew Annabella was going through. Even if he gave me the info I needed, I planned to leak the video to the press. He was supposed to look out for his clients, not help someone kidnap them.

"The governor's wife wanted a meeting with her."

Gabriel picked up his phone and made a call. He would get as much information from Brock as we needed. "Why would the governor's wife want a meeting? And there's a difference between requesting a meeting and kidnapping someone from work."

"It has something to do with the 23andMe DNA test she took."

I grabbed Annabella's purse and headed for the exit. Gabriel was on my heels, talking to Brock. We needed to get to a computer or a conference room. We decided to head back to the hotel and figure out our next plan.

Gabriel called Neal and had him meet us at the

hotel. The drive was quick. I couldn't stop thinking about what could be happening to her or why it had happened in the first place.

"WHY CAN'T anyone get me a conversation with the governor?" I glanced up at the wall clock. Annabella was taken an hour ago. Time seemed to be going at the speed of light.

Neal shifted in his chair. "Nate has ties to the governor. Maybe try him."

I couldn't help but grind my teeth. I was still pissed at what he'd put her through. But I needed to find out where they'd taken her.

Nate answered the phone on the first ring. "Annabella?"

"No, this is John. Someone took Annabella, and we need your help."

"Anything."

I ran my hand through my hair. "What can you tell me about the 23andMe test you and she took?"

"Not much. Our results came in. I had one of the secretaries print them, and I took them home. I hadn't looked at them yet. We'd planned to do it together, and then everything happened."

"Do you have access to the test right now?"

I heard him typing on the keyboard. "This can't be right."

"That she's the governor's daughter?" I paced back and forth inside the hotel room. It felt like the walls were closing in around me. What if I was too late? "If I had gone to the restroom with her, this wouldn't have happened."

Gabriel rested his hand on my shoulder. "Stop that train of thought, man. We will get her back."

"Nate, do you have an address or number for the governor?"

"Hold on a second." Nate placed the phone on hold. It felt like an eternity before he clicked back over. "The governor agreed to meet you at his house." Nate rattled off the address to the governor's house.

"This is dangerous. They kidnapped Annabella. I'm not waiting for the governor to show up. I'm going into the house no matter if he's there or not."

"Get her back. Please make sure she's okay.," Nate said. "I will meet you there." The line went dead.

"Hang on, Beautiful. I'm coming for ya," I whispered as I ran through the parking lot to our rented SUV.

~

ANNABELLA

The sound of two people screaming started to clear

the fog in my head. I tried to move my hands, but they were still tied down to a chair. I wasn't dead yet. The screaming became louder as I opened my one good eye. The other one was completely swollen shut. The room came into focus, and I noticed a new man in the room. The governor had shown up. Would he kill his own flesh and blood?

I was still in shock at finding out my mother had slept with the governor. How could she have kept my father's identity from me? It wasn't that I cared about him being the governor. I'd thought my father was dead all of these years. I had used the test to see if I could find his family and find out information about who he was.

"How could you do this, Isabella?"

"She will ruin everything. You had a daughter with that tramp back in school. I did this for us. You were never supposed to know."

The governor pounded his fist against the desk. "No. You did this for you. I'm not the one pushing to be in the White House. You are. This girl might be my daughter. How could you do this?"

"Water," I choked out. I had caked blood on my mouth, and the inside felt like sandpaper.

The man who was supposed to be my dad turned and walked toward me. He leaned down to untie my hands, when the crazy lady grabbed a pair of scissors from the desk and charged at him. I screamed, but my voice came out more like a whisper. He turned a second to late, and she stabbed him in the arm. My hands were still tied to the chair. I was helpless. I couldn't do anything to help him as blood ran down his arm.

"You've lost your mind, Isabella. What do you think is going to happen next?" He gripped his arm, trying to stop the bleeding.

The crazy lady started to pace back and forth. She kept mumbling to herself and running her hand through her hair. "I can make it look like she attacked you. When she found out you were her father and wouldn't pay, she came after you."

Governor Jackson sat in the office chair next to me. "It won't work. You know who she is. She doesn't need money."

"Why are you defending her? You're my husband."

The governor slowly pulled his phone out of his pocket. He didn't look down as he pressed a couple buttons. "Yes, I'm your husband. But if that test is right, she is my daughter. There is nothing you can do about this."

She stopped pacing, grabbed her glass off the desk, and threw it across the room. It shattered when it hit the wall. "When I proved to Trina you cheated on her, I never thought I would have to deal with the bitch again. Now I have to deal with her daughter."

"I never cheated on Trina."

The dumb bitch rolled her eyes. "You were always too stupid. I knew you wanted to get into politics. She wouldn't have been right for you, so I made her go away."

"Who else have you made go away?" His voice turned hard. "My mother didn't die in an accident, did she?"

"The stupid old lady found out I had an abortion and was going to tell you. I had to take care of her. You never saw what I had to sacrifice for us to get here."

The governor's arm was still bleeding, and his face was becoming ashen. I kept working at the ropes around my hands. I could feel the blood trickle down my wrist. But I needed to do something quickly, or we both might die.

I worked the rope back and forth, trying not to move too much. My dad's head started to bob.

"I can't go to jail," the crazy lady stated to the room.

I needed to keep her talking so I could buy us some more time. I needed to save us. There was no way John would figure out where I was.

My hand slipped a little through the ropes. I was getting close to getting them loose. "Isabella, you have to do something, or he's going to die. He's lost too much blood."

Her hair was no longer perfect. Strands stuck everywhere. She looked to where my dad was slumped over in the chair. Instead of coming over and trying to help him, she yanked the top desk drawer open and pulled out a gun.

"Killing us will not save you. My friends will know I didn't come here to kill him. I was taken off the set of a movie. They will search until they find answers."

"I will kill everyone who comes after me. I will not go to prison for that ungrateful bastard. He's in office because of me." She waved the gun around the room as she spoke.

My right hand came free. Isabella wasn't paying attention to me as I reached across and untied my other hand. My fingers tingled from finally getting circulation back into them. I had to fight through the pain. I didn't know if my dad was going to make it.

Isabella turned from looking out the window to see my hands untied. "No," she screamed, aiming the gun at my dad. "I will be the poor widow. I will make it look like you committed suicide. I will not go down for murder. I always win." Her finger went to the trigger.

I lurched my body from the chair to cover my father's. He couldn't die. I heard my name screamed from the doorway at the same time I felt the searing pain in my side. Chaos broke out. I heard two more gunshots. I waited for the pain to register, but nothing happened.

Someone grabbed me and tried to drag me off my dad. I hugged him tighter and screamed for the person to let me go.

"Beautiful, it's me. I need to look at you."

At the sound of John's voice, I let go, and Gabriel rushed to my dad's side.

John held me in his arms and pressed his hand to my wound. I screamed in pain. "I need to keep pressure on it. The doctor will be here in a second."

"Save my dad," I whispered before the room went dark.

18

JOHN

"Any changes?" Governor Paul Jackson asked. He had demanded to see his daughter the second he'd woken up in the ER. Instead of trying to argue with him, they'd let him up to her room. The hospital had wanted to run a couple of tests before they would release him, and he'd just finished his last test.

"No change," I said. "Has the doctor agreed to release you?"

He sat down in the chair next to Annabella's bed. His arm was in a sling from where he'd been stabbed. Annabella looked like she had gone ten rounds in a boxing match. Her right eye was swollen shut. Her pretty pink lips were puffy and swollen.

The governor reached over and grasped Annabella's hand. "I can go. I still can't believe she didn't tell me we had a daughter back in college. Annabella's mother was the love of my life. One day, she dumped me and said it was over." The older man glanced out the window and wiped his eyes.

No matter what Annabella tried to tell me, I would never leave her. I didn't care if it had only been a week. I knew she was the one. I'd already called Brock to tell him I planned to move to California. When he asked me to run a division of Blackwood Security out in California, I'd said yes immediately. Running one of the divisions would make it so I wouldn't have to go overseas as much.

The governor leaned back in his chair. "When are you going back to Florida?"

My mouth twitched. "I don't plan to leave Annabella. I will get an apartment out here and do whatever it takes to win her heart."

"I still can't believe she's my daughter. I missed all this time getting to know her."

Annabella's finger moved for a second, and I waited for her to open her pretty green eyes. "You need to stop thinking about the time you lost. There's no way to get it back. The only thing you can do is move forward and spend time with her."

Paul ran his good hand through his hair. "You know, when I was waiting to get my test done, my security came back and told me you work for Blackwood Security."

"I was in the same squad as the current owner."

"I've never heard anything bad about the merce-nary company. They only hire the best. I know I just found out I had a daughter, but I'm glad she's with you. I know she's protected."

"Are you planning on keeping her a secret?" When or if they decided to announce their relationship to the public, it would be on the cover of every magazine.

Paul shook his head. "No. I never wanted to run for president. That was Isabella's dream, not mine. Zack Turner does a good job."

I let out a sigh of relief. "That's good because Zeke Turner, the president's brother, works with us back in Ft. Lauderdale and is a close friend of the family."

"I have no doubt you will take good care of my daughter. I'm just hoping she will forgive me for what happened."

Annabella's eyes slowly opened. "I forgive you," she whispered. I reached over and grabbed her hand. She gave me a weak smile. "You don't need an apartment. You can stay with me."

The governor started to get up. "Annabella, your mom should be here with you. I'll leave until we have time to talk this out."

Annabella reached for her dad's hand. "Mom passed away seventeen years ago from cancer."

Paul sat back down in the chair. "I can't believe she didn't tell me about you. Your mother was the most amazing person in the world. You look so much like her."

"She was an amazing mom. I'm sorry I caused so much of an issue with Isabella. I really didn't know about the test. I promise I'm not after your money. Nate wanted to help me find out if I had any family on my dad's side still alive."

The governor scooted the chair up next to Annabella's bed. "You never have to apologize for doing that test. You made me the happiest man in the world. I can't believe I have a daughter. If you want, I would love to spend more time getting to know you. As for Isabella, we won't have to worry about her anymore. When you're ready, I'm here for you." Paul handed me his business card. "Call me when you want to meet for lunch." He leaned over and kissed Annabella on the forehead. "Get better, daughter. I can't wait to spend time with you." He quickly wiped his eyes and headed for the door. He stopped before he left. "I will take care of the media around Isabella. I don't want your name dragged through the press because of my crazy wife. Don't get me wrong—we will go to the press and let them know I have a daughter, but on our time, not theirs." The governor walked out the door and closed it behind him.

"Hey, Beautiful. I'm glad you're awake."

Tears streamed from her eyes. "You came for me."

I gently wiped her tears away. "I will always come

for you, but you need to stop getting yourself almost killed."

"I'll try. Are you really thinking about moving here? When you were talking to my dad, the words seemed so far away. Can you believe that the governor is my father? What about your job?"

I gripped her hand. "Brock offered me a job running a division of Blackwood Security out here in California, and I told him I would. We discussed that maybe the division should be more bodyguards for the rich and less jetting off to other countries to deal with pirates and terrorist organizations."

Annabella looked toward the door. "I like the idea of you taking less dangerous jobs. Did you kill Isabella?"

"There still might be a chance that I have to help the team out of Ft. Lauderdale every so often, and no, I didn't kill Isabella. One of the governor's bodyguards did." After I'd seen what she had done to Annabella, I wanted to unload a round into the bitch. "Gabriel called and told me they caught the other two men who kidnapped you. They were taken to jail. You never have to worry about them again, and now we know why someone was after you. We also have video footage of your manager helping. I sent it over to the sheriff."

"I never thought a DNA test would be so dangerous. As for my manager, I thought earlier today that it was time to find a new one. He hasn't done anything to help with my career. After this next movie, I'm going to have to start looking for a new manager."

A knock sounded on the door, and Daisy poked her head in. Neal and Aaron stood behind her. "Can we come in?"

"Yes," Annabella whispered. I handed her a cup of water. Her voice was hoarse from screaming earlier.

"Wow. What does the other guy look like?" Neal joked. I flipped the fucker off.

Neal sat in the chair by the window, and Daisy sat on his lap. Aaron stood next to them with his hand resting on Neal's shoulder.

"So with the person coming after Annabella dead, are you heading back to Ft. Lauderdale?" Aaron asked.

"Nope. I plan to stay out here. I might have to head back to Boston and talk with Addie about our mom. I know she said she had to head back to her family. She told her current family one of her cousins was sick and she was going to help them for a week."

Annabella tapped the side of the bed. "How is she flying by herself? I thought she had agoraphobia?"

I couldn't help but grind my teeth. "She's taking medicine and works with a psychiatrist. According to her, Henry, her new husband, is why she changed. It wasn't because of the two kids she left behind. I don't know why Addie hasn't kicked her out of her house. I don't want anything to do with the bitch. But Addie's going to need me there for her."

"You're going to have to go to Ft. Lauderdale to pick up your stuff. If I sent the private jet, would she get on it? We could all spend the weekend down in Ft. Lauderdale," Aaron said.

Flying on the private jet would expose Addie to fewer people. If Annabella was spending the weekend in Ft. Lauderdale with me, my sister might get on the plane to meet her in person. "I plan to call her tonight. I will ask her if she feels up to going."

We spent the next hour joking and laughing before Annabella fell asleep. Aaron pulled Daisy off Neal's lap. Nate stretched his arms. "You guys are welcome to come stay at the house if you want. Even if you don't come back on the plane with us, the house is yours to use," Neal said as he stood from the chair.

"Thanks, but I think we'll stay at the hotel until we find something."

Aaron pulled Daisy into his arms, "You're really staying out here?"

"I would go anywhere she wants me to. She's never getting rid of me. I plan to find an apartment and open a division of Blackwood out here."

Daisy came over and wrapped her arms around me. "I will never be able to tell you how much you and Sam rescuing me from my kidnapper five years ago means to me. I'm going to miss seeing you every day at Blackwood Security in Ft. Lauderdale. But my friend is getting a good man. Take care of her, John. She needs you." Daisy kissed my cheek then grabbed Neal and Aaron's hands and walked out the door.

The room was quiet after everyone left. I leaned back in the chair and watched Annabella sleep. I couldn't help but wonder how I had fallen for someone so fast. I'd never expected to see myself in a relationship. Now all I could do was wonder what tomorrow would bring.

Annabella's eyes fluttered open, and she tried to smile. "What are you thinking about so deep in thought?"

"I love you. I know it's early. You don't have to say anything back. I will be here for the long haul."

Annabella reached for my hand and squeezed it. "I don't have to wait. I feel the same way. I always laughed when I heard about people falling in love fast. But when it feels so right, why fight it?" She wiped a wayward tear away. "I love you, John."

I'd fallen for her the second I walked into the sheriff's station. She'd shown me so many times over the last week how genuine she was, and she was nothing like the tabloids made her out to be. She took time to talk to my sister whenever Addie called.

A couple of hours later, the doctor came and discharged Annabella.

19

JOHN

Annabella fell asleep on the car ride to the hotel. "Beautiful, you need to get up. We're at the hotel."

She slowly stretched in the seat next to me. I handed the valet the keys to the car and rushed to Annabella's side. "Anna, scoot over to the edge, and I can carry you inside."

I thought she might not let me carry her, but she scooted to the edge so I could wrap my arms around her and pick her up. She nuzzled her face into my chest so no one could see who she was. The press hadn't caught wind of what had happened yet, and we were trying to keep it from them if we could.

"You can put me down now," she said once the door to the elevator closed.

I clicked the button for the top floor. "I want you close."

She smiled. "I can stand close to you."

"You're stuck in my arms. I don't know if I will ever let you out of them. You scared me."

Annabella turned and kissed my neck then wrapped her arms around me and squeezed harder. "I promise not to have any more crazy stepmoms try to kill me."

I didn't answer her. The elevator door opened, and I headed straight for the room. I sat her down on the couch in the middle of the hotel room. "Do you want to take a shower?"

When Annabella nodded, I headed toward the bathroom connected to her room and started the shower to get the water nice and warm. We would need to rebandage her side. The bullet had grazed her, but luckily she hadn't needed stitches.

I walked back to the living room. Annabella was staring out the window.

"What's wrong?"

She shook her head and grabbed my hand. We walked back through the bedroom to the master bath. I tugged her into my arms and kissed the top of her head before I worked the thin white T-shirt up her body. Blood coated the sleeve and the back of her shirt.

"Join me," Annabella whispered as she worked my shirt over my head.

I wrapped my arms around her, pulled her into my body, and gently kissed her lips. Her lip and eye were still swollen. I wanted to kill the dumb bitch again for hurting her. I pulled back and placed a kiss on her nose. "Get undressed, Beautiful."

Annabella worked her jeans down her legs. I couldn't hold back a growl when I saw the bruises on her legs. Her body was black and blue from top to bottom.

When she finished removing her jeans, I quickly discarded my jeans and boxers. I grabbed her hand and led her to the shower.

I pulled Annabella under the waterfall shower head. The water rained down on us. I kept her wrapped in my arms, not wanting to let her go. A sob broke out from her throat. I ran my hand up and down her back as she let out the frustration from the past couple of weeks.

I grabbed a washcloth and put some soap on it. I slowly worked to wipe the blood off her body. It was a mixture of hers and her dad's. Her heart beat against my chest as I worked to get the blood off her arms. Our embrace wasn't sexual. It was healing from the day of turmoil. I was desperate for her to be in my arms.

The sob that escaped Annabella was heart-wrenching. "I d-didn't think you w-would find me." I pulled back and ran the cloth down her chest. She whimpered under the touch.

"I will always come for you." I turned her so her hair was under the spray. Then I grabbed the shampoo off the ledge and worked my fingers through her hair. She leaned her head forward and rested it on my chest. I rinsed the shampoo out and repeated the process with conditioner. I worked the lather up and down her body, stopping to kiss each bruise as I washed away the nightmare of the day. Once I washed and kissed every bruise on her body, I reached and turned off the water. A big, fluffy towel sat outside the shower, and I wrapped it around Annabella.

"Thank you," she told me quietly.

I grabbed the other towel and tied it around my waist. Then I snatched a small towel off the shelf and helped dry Annabella's hair. "Sit down on the toilet, and I will comb your hair." When she gave me a puzzled look, I said, "I had a twin sister I would do anything for. I know how to brush and braid a girl's hair."

I found Annabella's brush on the counter and slowly ran it through her blond locks. Her hair was long and reminded me of the times I'd done Addie's hair growing up. My heart hurt at the thought of Addie. She had been so excited to find our mother, and the woman didn't really want anything to do with us.

"All done. Stay here." I ran back to the bedroom and got one of my shirts from my bag. I came back and helped Annabella slip the shirt over her head. "You can finish up in here. I'll be in the bedroom." I left Annabella to brush her teeth.

I grabbed a pair of boxers from my bag and put them on before I climbed into bed and waited for her to come out. "Come here, Beautiful," I said when she finally emerged.

She walked over and climbed into bed with me. I rolled on my back, and Annabella snuggled up next to me, lying her head on my chest. She slowly ran her hands along my ribs. "Can you believe my dad is alive?"

I pulled her in closer to me. "How do you feel about finding him?"

She let out a chuckle. "It would have been nice to find out about him when I opened the paperwork Nate printed off for me."

"Do you think you'll talk to Nate again?"

Annabella didn't answer right away. "I will. I'm still mad at what he did. But we've been friends for years. In a few weeks, I will have lunch with him, and we can talk it out."

"You're a forgiving person. What do you think about coming back to Ft. Lauderdale for the weekend with me? We can try to get Addie to come too. Aaron mentioned we could send the jet to pick her up."

"I would love to go, and I can't wait to meet your sister."

EPILOGUE - JOHN

I reached down and picked up the chubby-cheeked baby tugging at my pants. Jessica and Brock's little boy, Jared, was six months old. Annabella and I had flown into Ft. Lauderdale for the weekend to spend time with friends and stop at Club Sanctorum for a night.

Jared reached up and tugged on my hair. Annabella reached over and pulled the little boy from my arms then rocked him back and forth. I couldn't believe we had been together for nine months already. She had just finished filming another movie and had a couple months off before the next one.

With her time off, she was helping me set up Blackwood Security in Los Angeles. We already had a list of clients who wanted to use our services, and we couldn't wait to expand. But this weekend was about catching up with friends.

Brock leaned down and kissed his little boy on the head. "Your sister has been picking up more cases to help us out."

Addie used work to deal with her anxiety. Our mom hadn't reached back out to her or me since visiting nine months ago. "She does that when she's stressed. Annabella and I are going to go visit her on Monday. I'm going to try and talk to her and see what's going on."

"Maybe we could send one of the guys up there and see if she falls for them," Brock joked.

I barked out a laugh. "I think your days of playing matchmaker are done. Why don't you worry about the business and stop meddling in people's lives?"

Annabella reached over and squeezed my leg. "If it weren't for Brock, we wouldn't be together."

"No, Nate is the one that started this. Brock used it to his advantage."

My longtime friend and boss smiled, grabbed his baby, and walked back over to Jessica and sat down. We were at Aaron and Neal's house in Ft. Lauderdale, sitting around the fire outside. It was nice to be around our friends. But I missed our home in Los Angeles. Annabella and Nate were on speaking terms. She hadn't completely forgiven him for what he'd done, but he had put his foot down with his family and let it be known that Pedro would be his partner.

Kat Ross, Aaron's sister-in-law, kicked her feet back. "You know, John, if you ever need an assassin, I'm always looking for jobs. Brock and Antonio don't let me kill anymore."

Her husband rolled his eyes. "Kat, I saw you drag a body across our lawn two days ago. Why do you have to feed the gators in the backyard?"

"Mommy, you fed the gators today," Antonio, Jr. chimed in.

"See? This is why I need assignments in other states. Everyone is up in my business," Kat grumbled and crossed her arms.

Antonio leaned over and pulled his wife into his arms.

Everyone laughed around the fire.

"I wish I could get my hands on Lily's ex-husband," Kat said. "He got out of jail last week, and we lost his trail."

Lily used to live in the women's shelter in Ft. Lauderdale. Her husband had gone after Kat and tried to kill her. Antonio and Kat had helped Lily escape to Houston, where she got a job working for Jacob Black, the owner of Pegasus Space.

Annabella leaned over and rested her head on my shoulder. "I love our life," she whispered.

"I love you." I leaned over and kissed her head. I couldn't wait to spend the rest of my life with her.

THE END

Click here to pre-order Lily's book, Pursuing Phoenix.

AUTHOR NOTE'S

White Hat Security Series

Hacker Exposed

Royal Hacker

Misunderstood Hacker

Undercover Hacker

Hacker Revelation

Hacker Christmas

Hacker Salvation

Nova Satellite Security Series
(White Hat Security Spin Off)

Pursuing Phoenix - Sept 1, 2019

Immortal Dragon

The Dragon's Psychic - July 9, 2019

The Dragon's Human - Oct 2019

Montana Gold (Brotherhood Kindle World)

Grayson's Angel

Noah's Love

Bryson's Treasure - Nov 2019

A Flipping Love Story (Badge of Honor World)

Unlocking Dreams

Unlocking Hope - Sept 10, 2019

Siblings of the Underworld

Hell's Key (Part of the Shadows and Sorcery Box Set)

Hell's Future - Aug 20, 2019

Visit linzibaxter.com for more information and release dates.
Join Linzi Baxter Newsletter at Newsletter

ABOUT AUTHOR

Linzi Baxter lives in Orlando, Florida with her husband and lazy basset hound. She started writing when voices inside her head wouldn't stop talking until the story was told. When not at work as an IT Manager, Linzi enjoys writing action-packed romances that will take you to the edge of your seat.

She enjoys engaging her readers with strong, interesting characters that have complex and stimulating stories to tell. If you enjoy a little (or maybe a whole lot) of steam and spice, don't miss checking out White Hat Security series.

When not writing, Linzi enjoys reading, watching college sports (GO UCF Knights), and traveling to Europe. She loves hearing from her readers and can't wait to hear from you!

Made in the USA
Las Vegas, NV
05 July 2022

51138945R00118